AT FIRST SIGHT

JOE PASCENTE

At First Sight

© 2020 by Joe Pascente

ISBN (Print): 978-1-09833-881-7
ISBN (eBook): 978-1-09833-882-4

Dedicated to all the lovers

&

the fighters

Chapters

CHAPTER 1

THE LONG WALK

I. A Shot in the Dark

Dorothy Hatch sat down, tangled in her wedding dress, on an oversized purple velvet chair having second thoughts. She was in a private dressing room, in the church where she was soon to be married. Her old-fashioned lace gown was the dress she had always pictured herself wearing at her wedding. It hugged her delicate body in all the right places, but something about the gown was just—off.

She wore a set of sparkling diamond earrings that reflected in the three-way mirror upended directly in front of her. Dorothy focused on her reflection. Makeup had been applied to her flawless skin, her dress had been buttoned along her lower back and her veil had been pinned in place. Wanting a few moments to herself, she left her bridesmaids in the bridal dressing room while she gathered her thoughts in the bride's dressing room. Not only did she require some personal alone time; she also needed sufficient amount of time to accomplish a covert matter.

Dorothy's light brown eyes gazed upon the three-way mirror, unfocused at first, but then her eyes caught the glimmer of her shimmering diamond earrings. She noticed her slender neck, and as her gaze travelled further down her left forearm, she couldn't help but stare at the two-inch needle plunged into her delicate skin. She had injected herself with the lightning-blue serum that was flowing freely from the syringe and into her veins.

Wow, what a rush...feels a bit like pins and needles.

3

The serum was now circulating in her bloodstream and there was no turning back. Dorothy hadn't ever associated herself with drugs of any kind. They had never agreed with her body, or mind. Taking an aspirin was usually out of the question for Dorothy Hatch; but, in this particular case, her curiosity got the best of her.

Dorothy had a mental picture of her fiancé in her head and thought about how swiftly they had fallen in love. Vance Richmond, the charming son of the Chicago Mayor, was an accomplished district attorney. It had only been a year prior when Vance met Dorothy through a mutual friend at a cozy teashop. And, it had been only six months ago when he had asked her to be his wife. Everything happened so suddenly, and lately, Dorothy was questioning everything about the life she had signed up for.

I don't feel any different. I thought I'm supposed to feel something...

Dorothy was confused by the lack of physical and neurological changes she assumed she would feel after injecting the drug into her body. Her perception of reality was exactly as it had been before the injection.

"Dorothy! Let's go, girl. We're minutes away from lining up!"

The maid of honor had begun to panic and tried budging the door open to the private dressing room, which was not opening due to Dorothy locking it behind her. With a startled gasp, Dorothy threw the empty syringe into a small trashcan beside the three-sided mirror. The label on the syringe had one bold word on the side, which read, **PURE**.

Dorothy gathered herself and opened the door with a theatrical smile painted on her face. Her bridesmaids saw a confident woman ready to walk down the aisle and marry the love of her life, even though Dorothy was secretly reeling with an extreme case of cold feet. One question kept shooting through her cluttered mind...one she couldn't answer, no matter how hard she tried...

Is Vance really my true love?

This question was the reason Dorothy injected herself with Pure, just moments ago. Dorothy watched her bridesmaids walk down the aisle to the echoing sounds of the church organ playing in the distance.

Her father was gleaming with pride and said, "You look so beautiful, Dorothy. I'm so proud of the woman you've become."

Clutching his gentle arm with her own, she whispered, "Thank you, Dad."

It was their turn to walk down the aisle. Through her veil, she could see everyone in her life whom she loved and cared so deeply for. Not only were her relatives and friends in attendance, but also many important political figures, due to her father-in-law being the Mayor of Chicago. And, all the way down the white linen aisle, stood her dashing groom, grinning with the sweetest smile on his cleanly shaven face. He stood tall and enchanted, watching the woman of his dreams walk down the aisle ready to be his wife. Dorothy kept questioning the drug she had just given herself in the private dressing room.

Where are the fireworks? When is this supposed to kick in?

Dorothy tried to hold in her alarmed energy, but unavoidably, she wasn't feeling the effects of Pure. She gazed into Vance's eyes, as she got closer to the wedding party standing at the front of the church. Her affectionate smile slowly began to fade. The room seemed to shrink in size and her blood pressure was rising at a rapid pace. Her stomach twisted in knots, as she couldn't hide her disappointment.

Maybe I got a bad batch of Pure... Or maybe...

Dorothy's father lifted the veil over his daughter's head and kissed her gently on the cheek, placing her shaky hands into Vance's. Dorothy managed to strike up a smile, seeing how excited Vance was to see his bride for the first time in her white lace gown. He whispered the words, "You're breath-taking," and with those simple words, Dorothy had a calming sense of relief that moved her into a blissful state.

Dorothy was upset with herself for doubting the love she had for the man she planned to be with from this day forward, even if the effects of Pure were non-existent.

After taking a few deep breaths, Dorothy could feel her cold feet warming up, especially as she held onto Vance's hands with the intention of never letting go.

But sometimes in life, things occur at the worst impeccable timing possible. Just as Dorothy started to relax, she peered over Vance's shoulder at the groomsmen behind him, and spotted Vance's cousin, Robert, whom she had only recently met in person, days before the wedding. Robert's eyes met Dorothy's, and in a whimsical instant, Dorothy's life altered significantly.

From Dorothy's perspective, the church and everyone standing inside, were nothing but a vast gray swirl of smoke. The only colorful light remotely visible to her was the gleaming illumination shining from Robert's essence. There was nothing in this universe but the two of them. Seeing fireworks was an understatement. It was as if Dorothy was in a hypnotic state of being, letting go of Vance's hands and leaping into Robert's arms. She mounted a kiss on his lips in their very first close embrace. The kiss was a breath of fresh air for these two strangers, in the stifling room of gasps and loud murmuring coming from every guest who wasn't utterly speechless.

"Dorothy—what the hell? What are you doing?" Vance questioned louder with every word, as he was quite the opposite of speechless.

All at once, Dorothy's world came rushing back around her, pulling her lips off of Robert's. She understood she was kissing her groom's cousin and knew this was a terrible occurrence, however, she didn't regret it in the slightest. She knew, the drug—Pure—had worked beyond a reasonable doubt. She looked upon Robert, and knew with every fiber in her being, he was the one true love of her life. It was a damn shame it had to happen this way, but what could a girl do?

Spinning around, Dorothy explained, "I took it, Vance. I know we agreed we wouldn't, but I just couldn't go through with marrying you without knowing for sure." She hadn't let go of Robert's hand while she tried to make sense of it all.

"You took Pure? I thought you told me you didn't need a damn 'love drug' to tell you whom you loved! You promised it was me!" Vance shouted, as the echoes from the perfect acoustics of the church scattered his words from one corner to the other.

"I was...I mean, I wanted it to be you...it just...isn't."

Dorothy looked into Vance's eyes and saw the tears forming, as he whispered, "But we made a promise."

Robert stepped beside Dorothy and put his arm around her waist. He looked remarkably similar to Vance, but wore glasses and had a full beard.

He knew he had to speak up and explain himself as well, saying, "I took Pure six months ago, Vance. I told you about it, remember? I broke up with my girlfriend when we felt the spark was gone. Pure's effects are *always* mutual. I couldn't possibly dismiss it now that I've seen Dorothy. She's the one."

"No, Robert!" Vance shouted. "This isn't love...it's just an altered perception of reality! You two don't even know each other! Do you know her favorite flower? Or the way she likes to be cuddled? Or any detail about the person she is? How could you say this is love?"

No one in the church could blame Vance for being as outraged as he was. Hell, neither Dorothy nor Robert could even blame him. It didn't make any logical sense, but Pure wasn't a logical drug. Indeed, it was a drug that altered perception, but only when one person came into contact with another person that was -supposedly, and always mutually—the love of each other's lives. The drug was triggered by the senses. Sight, being the number one trigger; but sense of smell and touch worked just as well—in the case of some blind people.

Dorothy and Robert didn't take long to exit from the church, hand in hand, after this awkward situation. Dorothy apologized and scurried out of the church without ever looking back. As the guests stayed in their seats, not knowing what their next move should be, they watched Vance sulk down the aisle with his dad's arm around his shoulders. They walked down the aisle towards the church's front entrance.

Vance sat down gently on the church steps and his father stood beside him. Vance's mind was racing and he was hoping this was all a nightmare he was going to wake up from soon. He watched his almost-bride get in his cousin's car and pull out of the church parking lot. Vance spotted Dorothy's bouquet of flowers on the church steps and kicked them across the stairs. Of course, this was the moment several news station cameramen flipped their cameras on and captured the entire tantrum.

The shocking incident of the Mayor's son being left at the church was on every local news station that night. Every day, for the past 21 months—since the creation of Pure—there were news stories associated with the ambitious love drug. The stories ranged from good to bad to the fairly odd. With titles such as: "82 Year-Old Woman Travels in Hot Air Balloon Searching for Her True Love," to "High School Students Drop Out to Find Their True Loves," to "Bride Uses Pure, Only to Fall in Love With Groom's Cousin."

Evidently, Pure was a blessing and a curse to all the romantics who believed in the possibility of true love. Many people lost hope finding someone to call their own…their soul mate…the love of their life. And Pure gave them the opportunity to find this special someone. It seemed as though love stories weren't just in Disney movies anymore; people could have their happily ever after, if only they could lock eyes with their true loves, after taking the shot, filled with the essence of Pure.

Geneco Inc. was the company that owned the rights to Pure. The scientist who created the drug was now quite famous because of the worldwide phenomenon it had become.

Dr. Angela Haven had studied genetics and biochemistry, getting her doctorate at Yale University. She was a well-accomplished doctor as well as a brilliant scientist. To anyone who knew Angela, it was no wonder she had developed this drug, but as great as her discovery was, it irrefutably came with a steep price.

II. A Breath of Fresh Air

Dr. Angela Haven had been under water for 45 seconds and counting. She was trying to stay stationary on the sandy floor of the Pacific Ocean. Angela enjoyed the current of the ocean swaying her body back and forth, inches at a time. The ocean was her "happy" place. It had been ever since she was a young child. She could always count on going under water and escaping any problem in her life.

These days, she used the ocean to escape the constant noise that rattled her head on a daily basis. The noise, being the screaming voices at the many press conferences she had been apart of recently, causing a deafening unrest for Angela.

As an alternative, the quiet sound of the water rushing above her head was precisely what she needed. Taking a handful of the ocean's sand and letting the grains slowly spill out of her fingers was part of Angela's meditation. Angela looked up to the surface of the water, watching the dancing sunlight scatter around the ripples of the waves that cascaded above her. The oxygen in her lungs was depleting and as she blew bubbles out of her mouth, she pushed off the sandy floor, propelling out of the water to inhale a mouthful of fresh summer air.

The warm California rays of sunlight hit her water-soaked face while she caught her breath. She opened her mint-green colored eyes, which had a permanent squint from the intense July sunlight. Angela was quite comfortable in the water, growing up as a competitive swimmer through her college days. She excelled in the backstroke, learning this skill as a young girl in her backyard pool. The rest of her free time as a medical student was spent studying, or reading the many books her father owned, as he was a doctor himself.

It had been over 2 years since Angela had finally finished developing a serum that was intended to help previously abused gorillas face their fear of intimacy, so they could mate without worry of being physically abused. The studies were quite effective and quickly became rather fascinating to the scientific world. Angela's company, Geneco Inc., fought hard and steadfast to begin human trials, which inevitably led to the impacting development of finding one's true love. Pure was a happy accident for Angela and her team, and was now, a multi billion-dollar goldmine for Geneco.

Angela had been thoroughly surprised the serum she had developed was fast becoming one of humanity's greatest innovations. For someone who had practically given up on love, it was quite ironic that Angela had made this tremendous discovery in her 30's.

Angela swam to the shallow sandbar with ease and was nosily observing all the people tanning on the beach. She pushed her wet, shoulder-length, wavy light-brown hair away from her eyes and walked towards the shore. The red bikini she wore clung to her skinny frame in all the right places. Her model-like figure was due to a combination of swimming, good genetics from her mother's side, and ingesting nothing but cups of green tea during long days in the Geneco laboratory. To any outsider, Angela had it all - looks, brains, and talent. She truly led a blessed life.

The red nail polish on her toenails was now covered in sand as she kicked it around walking back to her towel, plopping down on her flat stomach.

She was lying there listening to the effortless sounds of the ocean and the many seagulls squawking, letting the beach inhabitants know they were hungry for snacks. The water dropped off her body onto the beach towel as her wet hair covered her peripheral vision.

If only everyday could be this relaxing...

Angela thought about how hectic her life had become since Pure had turned out to be such a household topic of discussion. People were obsessed with the drug and she couldn't break away from being caught in the middle of the chaos that came along with it. She had more money now than she could've ever dreamt of. But Angela wasn't the type of person that needed money to be content; she was happiest when she had scientific research to do, or even some time to herself.

Down the beach, there was an obese, pale woman reading a book in a beach chair. She was about 20 yards away from Angela, dressed in a navy pants suit and large black sunglasses. This woman seemed a bit out of place here on the hot sandy beach, but Angela didn't pay much attention to this woman, as she wasn't behaving oddly, except for being dressed for a business meeting on a beach. Angela checked her phone realizing she had 15 missed calls and 107 emails in only a half-hour's time.

She knew she needed to head home and get some work done. The phone calls and email messages were a constant part of her life now. Not only were the board members at Geneco Inc. always demanding new tests and data from her, but she was also getting requests by the press. They all wanted to interview the woman who had changed the world's outlook on love.

She packed up the few items she brought to the beach — her car keys, her cellphone, sun tan lotion, and a trashy celebrity magazine. Putting on some tiny jean shorts and a white sleeveless t-shirt over her red bikini, she headed toward her new energy efficient car that she had parked down the road. It wasn't anything fancy, but it was one of the newest purchases she had made since she had come into her new wealth.

Walking on the soft warm sand, Angela noticed the strange pale woman dressed in her navy pants suit also stood up, glaring in her direction, taking fast-paced steps following Angela's foot trail.

Angela didn't think much about this, until she heard the swooping sounds of someone's footsteps drudging through the sand closely behind her. Gripping onto her keys, Angela pressed the unlock button to her car and walked briskly over to the driver's side fumbling with her beach bag filled with her belongings. She didn't need to look behind her to know the strange woman was getting closer by the second. It was as if she could feel the woman's eyes burning a hole through the back of her head.

Angela was a foot away from the driver's side of her car when she heard a loud BANG!

The pale woman slammed her fist on the rooftop of Angela's car, causing her to drop her keys in fear. The woman was standing on the passenger side of the car.

"Hey! You're *her*, aren't you?" The woman shouted in a raspy voice, with the distinct smell of gin and cigarettes on her breath. And that was saying something as she was on the other side of the car.

"Excuse me?" Angela asked, stepping a foot backwards. She knew this strange woman had recognized her and didn't want any trouble from this drunken lady.

Angela bent down to pick up her keys and watched the woman's bare feet making her way around the car closer to her. Feeling a bit flustered by this woman, Angela began to open the door before she came any closer, but the woman pushed the front door shut as she made her way around.

"You're the doctor who created Pure, are you not?"

Angela rummaged through her bag searching for the only form of protection she could use on this lady, in case things escalated into a scary confrontation.

"Please, leave me alone. I don't know who you think I am but I just want to get home." Angela was concerned for her safety, but she was also pissed off she couldn't find the one item in her bag she needed.

Where's that damn pepper spray? Why do I have so many packs of gum?

While Angela was searching for her pepper spray, this woman was shouting in her face.

"Your drug made my husband leave me for another woman! We were so happy until *your* damn drug came into our lives! How could you do this to us? How could you do this to *me*?"

Finally, Angela's hand felt the pepper spray bottle and she pointed it at the woman's face. The woman backed up and stopped shouting immediately.

"Get out of my face, lady! I didn't make your husband leave you. I'm sorry it happened but that's life! Sometimes things don't happen the way you intend them to. Now, back the hell up!"

Angela was sweating bullets, as she had never been confronted this close in person by anyone accusing her of turning their life upside down because of Pure. Sure, she had the many online trolls accusing and threatening her as of late, but never in person like this incident.

She managed to open the front door of her car and step inside. She threw the pepper spray on the passenger seat, then quickly locked the doors and buckled her seat belt. The angry woman was now standing in front of Angela's car, fiddling around with something inside her purse. Angela started her car and put the gear shifter in reverse, just as the strange woman pulled out a small handgun and pointed it at Angela's windshield.

Angela froze. She looked at this woman's sunglasses and back at the gun pointed at her. Before Angela could even duck, the woman pulled the trigger and shot the windshield.

The windshield cracked around the bullet hole that barely missed Angela's right ear. Ducking down instantly after the gunshot, Angela screamed out and accidentally hit the gear shifter to the drive position, stepping on the gas pedal. The car sped off in a forward motion, hitting the frantic woman in the legs, knocking her backwards into the sand lining the parking spaces. Angela kept driving even though she heard the crazy woman—who tried to shoot her—screaming about her injured foot.

Angela had limited time to react as she pulled away at rapid speed, dodging oncoming traffic. And then she heard it again; another gunshot hit the left taillight of her car. She screamed again, all the while keeping her head ducked down trying to look over the steering wheel in a panicked fright. She was now driving 65 mph, making her way down the road to get far away from the crazy woman she had narrowly escaped from.

Angela kept driving as fast as she could, wiping the tears from her eyes, all the while hyperventilating from the shocking experience that had just occurred. Once she felt she had driven far enough from the beach, she pulled over to the side of the road and cried into her shaking hands. She screamed out in fright and couldn't stop the tears from falling down her face. She looked down at her lap and there were tiny particles of glass scattered along the console of her car, as well as in her wet hair from the windshield's bullet hole.

Dr. Angela Haven's life had been turned upside down. She reported the crime and waited for the police to show up at her home. Angela knew her life would never be the same. She wasn't safe from anyone anymore. This was the moment she thought of Jeremy—her ex-fiancé, who was once the love of her life. It's funny how quickly things can change, as he wasn't in her life at all anymore. In fact, there wasn't anyone special in her life. Angela felt more alone than ever before.

III. This Way to Sway

At first glance, one wouldn't give much notice to the Los Angeles jazz club called, *Sway*. It wasn't much to look at from the red brick exterior, but that's what held a certain mystique to it. The brawny doorman was intimidating, standing in between the front door and the red velvet rope, creating a presence of exclusivity and prestige. Massive sunglasses and a broken-in fedora hat hid his extremely tan face, keeping the riffraff out of this very private sanctuary.

Most nights, there was a list and if your name wasn't on it, you were wasting your time standing in line. On this particular night, standing at the front of the line was the Mayor of Chicago, Harold Richmond, alongside his personal assistant and best friend, Henry Webster.

It had only been a couple of weeks since Harold's son's wedding fiasco. For those past two weeks, Harold had to watch his son fall into a downward spiral. Sleeping all day, every day, Vance was heartbroken and felt as if he'd never get over the pain of losing Dorothy to his cousin. Vance's father didn't like to see his son in such a sad state-of-being and he knew something must be done about his situation.

That's why Harold and his personal assistant flew halfway across the country to LA to come to this particular jazz club. Harold made damn sure they were on the list tonight. He had a stern look on his face, pushing the people in line out of his way, while Henry followed closely behind. The people waiting in line hollered at him to get to the back of the line, but they didn't realize Harold had a special meeting planned.

He reached the front of the line and gave the overly muscular doorman his name. The doorman used an earpiece device to inform the owner of *Sway*, his personal guests were here. Seconds later, the robust doorman unhooked the red velvet rope and let Harold and Henry in. The music coming from inside was loud and the entryway was so dimly lit, the only thing Harold and Henry could see was the section for coat check and two draping violet velvet curtains as the main entryway inside the lounge.

There were two levels to *Sway*. The main level had a dark, but vibrant, ambiance with low-key lighting and black and white pictures of classic jazz musicians who started the jazz revolution back in the 1920's. Red suede booths lined the walls and scattered tables and chairs filled the rest of the quaint club. A dimly lit stage was the center of focus on the back wall across from the main bar. The jazz band was on their last song before their intermission. The bar area was decently filled with dressed up patrons and some Hollywood elite. The crowd was now waiting in anticipation for the next gig to start as the music died down and the lights on the stage turned off completely.

Rumor had it *Sway* was actually a drug front for the owner. This rumor was, of course, just a rumor. But just because this particular rumor was false, didn't mean there wasn't some truth among the many whispers about *Sway*. The jazz club was indeed a front, but not for drugs; it was a front for a group of specialized black ops assassins using the basement level as their secret facility.

The basement level could only be reached by use of a hidden elevator that was behind the bookshelf in the owner's office on the main level. Only the group of specialized black ops assassins was allowed in the basement, along with the owner of *Sway*—who was also the group's mission leader— and went by the name of Duke Harrington.

As soon as Harold and Henry walked into the bar through the velvet curtain, a tall slender man greeted them with a simple nod signaling to follow him. They followed him closely, making the long walk through the club. This tall skinny man looked a bit out of place with his black-framed glasses and red mohawk hair cut. As the lights on the stage faded back on, everyone in the club became perfectly silent.

Standing behind the microphone was a petite, gorgeous Hawaiian woman wearing a sparkling silver mini cocktail dress, glimmering in the soft glow of the stage lights. She gripped the microphone with her right hand, and started singing a soft blues number with just her vocals. The band walked on the stage one by one and accompanied her singing to a soft tune that hypnotized the crowd.

This attractive singer made eyes with Harold as he passed by. He was quite captivated by her ruby red lips and her sensual voice. Henry pushed Harold forward, as the tall skinny man took the two men through a back door, close to the stage. They entered a thin hallway and walked a short way down to Duke's office.

It was only a couple minutes before Harold was escorted through Duke's office door, as the tall skinny man addressed Henry, letting him know he could wait outside until their meeting was over.

"But, I don't leave Harold's si—"

Harold grabbed his friend's shoulder, "Henry, it's all right. It'll be a short meeting with Mr. Harrington," Squeezing tightly onto his shoulder. "Wait here."

The tall skinny man shut the door behind Harold and stood guard while Henry cracked his knuckles in frustration.

Harold entered the old-fashioned office that smelled of cigars and potpourri and right away, Duke stood up to introduce himself.

"You must be Harold Richmond," he said with a puff of his cigar. "I'm Duke Harrington, we spoke on the phone earlier this week. Shall we get down to business?"

The two men shook hands and took their seats across Duke's Italian crafted wooden desk. His office resembled the interior of the club, with opaque lighting and black and white pictures on the walls. Duke was well into his fifties, but looked a bit older due to his smoking and drinking lifestyle that he had become accustomed to over the past 30 years. His slick black hair was receding, but he was in decent shape, filling out his grey and white pinstriped suit. He smelled of old spice and smoke.

"Thank you for taking the time to meet with me," Harold said while unbuttoning his suit jacket to get more comfortable. "It wasn't easy getting a hold of a man in your position. I had to go through many associates to find someone who could potentially help me with my family's…burden."

The cigar smoke swirled around Duke's dark eyes, causing a light vapor in the office air.

"As I told you on the phone, I heard about what happened to your son and I'm sorry your family is going through such a distressing ordeal. What can I do to help with your situation, Mr. Richmond?"

For the next few moments, Harold's temper was barely under control, as he explained what caused the grand catastrophe that was his son's "almost" wedding. A few times throughout Harold's ranting, Duke had to settle Harold down, to fully understand what he could do for him.

"To keep this succinct, I want this woman dead." Harold sputtered these words through his tight jaw.

"Dorothy, you mean? The woman who left your son at the altar?"

"No," Harold muttered. "Dorothy caused my son terrible heartache. She's now with my nephew, Robert. Apparently they are happy with one another. So I can't blame her for the effects of Pure. And, I know Vance wouldn't want Dorothy dead. She's not the one I want put to rest."

"Spill it then, Mr. Mayor. Which woman are we talking about here?"

"The woman who created that *damn* love drug. Angela Haven! She deserves what's coming to her for causing such devastation in everyone's lives. Do you know how hard it is to see my son act like a zombie because of this psychotic woman's drug? She needs to pay for this! Now, did I fly halfway across the country to see the right man for the job, or not?"

As Duke contemplated this proposal, he thought about his life's journey and knew almost instantly he was the right man for the job. Duke had put together a specialized team seven years ago and they had made large sums of money for an assortment of jobs. Duke signed his team up for the missions he knew they could handle without any hiccups, even if that meant assassinating important figureheads, like Dr. Angela Haven.

Looking Harold dead in the eye, Duke wrote down a price and slid it across his desk into Harold's hand.

"You came to the right man. My team and I will have the deed done in a matter of days." Duke put his hand out to shake on the deal, as Harold looked over the amount this would cost him.

"See that you do, Mr. Harrington," Harold said, shaking Duke's hand. "See that you do."

Harold stood up and took an envelope out of his coat pocket filled with cash, turning his back to Duke, he counted and replaced the proper amount of bills into the envelope, and then placed it back on the desk sliding it towards Duke. The amount inside the envelope was half; and he'd get the other half when the job was done, which was all part of the agreement.

Meanwhile, Henry was leaning against the hallway wall with his eyes shut listening to the sweet sounds of the beautiful woman singing a more upbeat song on the stage. Harold hustled out of Duke's office hastily.

"Let's go."

Harold and Henry made their way through the tables in the main lounge, as the pretty woman walked off the stage making her way to the bar. The room was still applauding and chattering, enjoying their lavish cocktails. Moments later, the sounds of another jazz band began to fill the room with some mellow mood music.

Harold left *Sway* feeling a sense of relief, knowing he was doing a solid favor for his son and the rest of the world by hiring Duke and his team of specialists for this imperative job.

Back inside *Sway*, the beautiful Hawaiian singer walked up to the bar. Turning to face the crowded club, she leaned her back up against the bar adjusting the bow in her hair.

The handsome bartender asked, "What'll you have, babe?"

"The usual. And you don't get to call me *babe* anymore, Ace."

Ace made her the usual drink that agreed with her, a whiskey ginger, as he smirked to himself thinking...

Was she always this cold?

The bartender, Ace, tended bar when he wasn't on black ops missions. He was part of Duke's elite team, as the sharp shooting sniper. Ace was his codename because he was an ace in the hole when it came to shooting. He was in his mid thirties, with dark handsome features and the lightest brown eyes. His crew cut hairstyle fitted him well, matching the scruff on his chiseled face. If he wanted, he could've had a career in modeling, but he enjoyed his work—shooting people for large sums of money.

The beautiful singer's codename was Bows, because she usually had at least one bow in her long black hair. She was the diversion for most of their missions because her beauty was quite entrancing and distracting. Not to mention she was quite deadly with a blade.

Ace clinked glasses with Bows as they both took a swig of their drinks. They sat there conversing with one another, making casual small talk, until it was closing time and everyone had left the cozy club.

The large doorman came back inside and took a seat next to Bows. He was also apart of the special ops team and his code name was Boulder, due to his large stature. He ordered his beer of choice and chugged it down in less than 30 seconds. Wiping the beer from his full black beard he squinted at the television. He didn't join in on Ace and Bow's conversation; instead, he changed the channel from behind the bar and watched ESPN highlights, spinning his fedora around his finger.

The tall skinny man with glasses and the red mohawk walked up to the seat next to Boulder. His code name was Worm, due to his long lanky body and the fact that he could hack into any computer system. He was about to sit down, but from the look Boulder gave him, Worm moved two seats over.

The four members of the team sat at the bar and waited for Duke. He informed them they needed to be here tonight because he had a meeting with a potential client. Duke walked up to the bar moments later, and Ace had a dirty martini ready for him.

"Where's your brother, Boulder?" Duke asked, after taking a large sip of his martini.

"He said he'd be running late. He had a lot of unpacking to do at this one's apartment." Boulder said nodding in Bows' direction.

Boulder knew this comment would cause some tension in the room between Bows and Ace. The two had broken up a while ago, but Bows had moved on faster than Ace thought possible, by dating Boulder's brother. He was also a member of Duke's team, and his code name was Rocky. He wasn't as big and bulky as his fraternal twin brother, but he was still a large muscular man, so the codename Rocky fit him well.

Bows quickly changed the subject and asked, "So, do we have a new target?"

"I wanted to wait for Rocky, but who knows when he'll get his dumb ass in here. Our new client wants the job done this week. Our target is a high profile woman that has been in the spotlight for the last year. We've all seen her TV interviews and it's not going to be the easiest mission we've encountered, but we always accomplish what we set out to do, no matter how difficult the circumstances seem to be. Our target's name is, Dr. Angela

Haven. It's a shoot to kill operation; pretty standard, but let's head downstairs and get this set up in pre-ops."

Ace immediately perked up when he heard the target's name. He made eyes with Bows and a second later, they both turned away from one another. This woman wasn't just famous around the world; she had changed their lives indirectly.

As the team made the long walk down to the hidden headquarters of *Sway*, Rocky pulled into the parking lot and sat in his beat up truck for a minute, smoking a joint. He knew he was late, but what was a few minutes more, as these "meetings" lasted unnecessarily too long for him. He switched on the radio and listened to a news report about an attack earlier today on the doctor who created Pure. He scoffed and shut the radio off finishing the last bit of his joint. He exhaled the smoke out of his window and chuckled to himself, saying "Crazy bitches."

Rocky took a second to use eye drops on his bloodshot eyes, knowing Bows didn't approve of his smoking habit. He was a stockier shorter version of Boulder—but his beard didn't come in as full and his eyes weren't as beady. He usually spent too much time doing his hair most days and had impeccably white teeth. He complimented Bows quite well, as couples go, being a few inches taller than her and just the right rugged look. He placed a piece of gum in his mouth and headed inside *Sway*, ready for his next adventure as part of Duke's team of assassins.

After seven years of missions, he realized the team didn't have a name they called themselves. Maybe it was because he was a bit high at the moment, or maybe it was always in his nature to think about these types of things, but Rocky contemplated various names—the Inevitables, Band of Boulders, Rocky and the Bandits—but nothing stuck.

As he walked to Duke's office, ready to go down the secret elevator, he thought maybe there was a reason Duke didn't have a special name for the team. Rocky felt it was already a bit unnecessary to give each of them code names like Rocky, Bows and Ace. Duke never revealed the true identities of his team to the rest of the staff at *Sway*. The rest of the servers and bartenders only knew them by their code names and knew better than to ask questions about their personal lives.

Rocky had made it to the elevator and as it was slowly creeping down, he wished he had time to light up another joint before going down. He was excited to see Bows, but he was also a bit paranoid she'd know he was high. He wasn't in the mood to see the rest of the crew, but they'd gone a few months without any missions so he was in need of the substantial paycheck.

The elevator doors opened and he was in the control room of *Sway*. It always reminded Rocky of the bat cave because of the low light and the numerous projected images on the many computer screens. Worm was explaining his systematic approach to this mission while the other crewmembers sat around the table. They all peered over in Rocky's direction as he entered the room.

"You're late." Duke muttered, his cigar hanging out of the side of his mouth.

"My bad. There was this crazy news story about that scientist lady who created Pure."

"You don't say…"

CHAPTER 2

WHAT COULD GO WRONG?

I. Her Kevin Costner(s)

Angela sat wilted over her desk holding her drowsy head up with one hand, while the other held onto a lukewarm cup of coffee. She was unaware a few strands of her wavy brown hair were stuck to the inside of her cup. Completely exhausted from the last few days of her whirlwind life, she was continually nodding off at work.

She was supposed to be developing other compound prospects for her drug, Pure, but she wasn't in the right state of mind. Her mint-green eyes were encircled by an enflamed reddish sclera, which matched with her disheveled hairdo that was in a loose bun on the top of her head. There were other scientists scurrying about in the lab, working on their own formulas as well as helping Dr. Haven with Pure.

Dr. William Rayne, the CEO of Geneco Inc., was also walking about the lab. He spotted Angela slumped over at her lab desk and understood her zombie-like behavior entirely. He walked over quietly and placed his hand on Angela's upper back, gently stirring her from the semi-sleep state she was in.

Angela quickly sat up tall and wiped the tiny bit of drool forming at the side of her mouth.

"I'm sorry, I just can't keep my eyes open today, Will."

"It's understandable after the last few days you've had. It's obvious you haven't been sleeping well. Why don't you take some time off? Find a private island and get away from everything. Hell, I'll join you. I need a vacation too."

Angela gave William a weak smile and continued to stare across the sizeable lab she spent most of her career existing inside. The fluorescent glow of the lights, which were humming above, cast an unflattering dull light on both of them. Angela held onto a vial of Pure and examined it bringing it close to her face. The vial held the lightning-blue serum, which seemed to glow ever so slightly under these lights.

"Every time I start to drift off, I see that woman's face. She was just so... angry, but also, so sad. I keep myself from falling asleep because I can't go another night waking up screaming. My life has become so..."

Angela wiped her eyes before any tears could fall down her cheeks. She gave Will a half-cocked smile, wanting to make sure he knew she was all right; even though she was far from it. Will knew better, of course, working with Angela for 7 years now. She wore her emotions on her sleeve and wasn't ashamed of it. Geneco was a large corporation and Angela's innovative drug had propelled the company to new heights. He would do anything for her, including protecting her any way he was capable.

Will opened his arms for Angela and she begrudgingly gave him a much-needed hug. She rested her head on his shoulder, but not for long. She knew Will had a bit of a crush on her, but he would never admit it openly, as he was her boss. It wasn't that he was a bad looking guy, but she saw him as a friend and superior. That's as far as her feelings went. But at this moment, she really did appreciate the sentimental hug.

"So I need to tell you something," Will began to say. "I know you were against the idea when I first brought it up, but you know me; I do what's in the best interest of my company, especially, when it concerns you. With that being said, you don't have to worry about your safety any longer."

Will was still hugging Angela as close as he could without being creepy. However, Angela didn't like the sound of what he had just said. She backed away from Will with a perplexed look on her face.

"You didn't do what I think you did, *right*?"

Will nodded his head towards the glass windows that were between the laboratory and the hallway beside them, and standing there—like two solid unmovable statues—were two fit men, dressed in matching black suits with their arms behind their backs.

"These two gentlemen are your personal bodyguards, Angela. They both come highly recommended and I feel much better knowing you will be safe in their hands. No one will get close enough to hurt you."

Angela was speechless. She looked upon these two strangers that were hired to protect her from any harm that could potentially come her way; yet, these two men were still strangers to her.

She put one foot in front of the other and walked closer to the window inspecting the two bodyguards. The two men couldn't be more dissimilar from one another. From first glance, she could see the bodyguard standing to the left was an older gentleman in his late forties, with the beginning signs of gray streaks in his jet-black hair. He wore a cheesy grin that displayed his crooked upper teeth.

Angela then observed the other bodyguard to his right. He was a good looking black man, closer to Angela's age, mid-thirties, with an athletic body. He wasn't smiling, so there were no sign of his pearly whites at all. He was all business. He came off stuffy and arrogant from Angela's point of view. Of course, this was just a first impression through the glass window of her lab. He seemed overconfident; or maybe that was just his sophisticated nature, looking directly into Angela's eyes. His gaze trapped Angela into a standstill, and she found herself unable to look away from his gaze.

"Are you upset with me?" Will asked.

Looking back to Will's puppy dog eyes, Angela thought for a few seconds how she felt about this. She looked back to the bodyguard with the strong gaze, but he was now conversing with his partner discussing something that seemed rather urgent.

"I'm not upset…I appreciate the concern, but I can take care of myself. This is completely unnecessary, Will. It's a waste of the company's money."

"First off, don't worry about this company's financial costs. It's really no trouble at all. And secondly, a crazy Karen almost shot you in the face earlier this week. I didn't want to tell you this, but we've also been receiving some death threats addressed to you. So, in all retrospect, it *is* necessary."

"What? How many death threats is *some*?"

"Enough to warrant hiring these gentlemen for your protection. They're the best money can buy. I wouldn't have it any other way. Let me introduce you to them."

Angela was apprehensive to follow Will outside the lab and into the hallway to meet her bodyguards. She felt quite embarrassed looking the way she did at this moment. She was still half-asleep, wearing her lab attire and her hair was a mess. She wanted to take the lab coat off before meeting the bodyguards, but William grabbed her hand, dragging her behind him.

Will introduced the first agent.

"Angela, I'd like you to meet Steven Hicks," The older bodyguard shook Angela's hand with a firm grip. "And…I'm sorry, I don't recall your first name, Mr. Jacobi?"

"It's just Jacobi." The overconfident bodyguard answered, holding his hand out to shake Angela's.

"So, what, you're like the *Beyoncé* of bodyguards?" Angela asked, shaking his hand with curiosity.

As soon as she asked this question she immediately regretted it realizing it was a terrible dad joke. Angela didn't always have the best social skills, seeing as she'd rather read books and be on her own, instead of interacting with kids her age.

Jacobi finally smiled at Angela's bad dad joke.

"You can say that, although I don't know if my dance moves are up to par."

"Pleasure to meet you both." Angela said.

"Likewise, Dr. Haven," Mr. Hicks stated. "When you're all through here, we'll drive you to your home to pick up your essentials and then we'll make our way to the hotel." Angela was perplexed seeing she was not privy to this plan before meeting these men.

"Hotel? Wait, why are we going to a hotel?" she asked.

Will clarified what Mr. Hicks had tried to explain.

"One of the death notes we received yesterday included your home address. Your home isn't safe to stay at right now. We'd all feel much better about this delicate situation if you stayed at a hotel for a week, or two, while the police investigate these death threats."

Angela's face couldn't hide anything. She had one of those expressive faces that showed her every emotion, and right now, her lips were pursed, her eyebrows were scrunched, and her eyes were squinting at Will, appalled at the idea she had to relocate from her cozy beachside home. No, she didn't like this idea one bit.

"I don't care about the death threats. I'm not leaving my home."

"Well, no offense, Dr. Haven, but we were hired to protect you and that requires getting you away from any potential danger," Mr. Hicks paused and looked at his partner for reassurance. "Someone, or possibly a group of individuals, knows where you live and even with our protection, we don't feel comfortable letting you stay there for the time being. Please trust us, we will be staying in the presidential suite at a very exclusive hotel."

Angela's face wasn't budging. She wasn't on board with this plan of action.

"Besides, I really don't fancy sleeping in our car outside your house. This works best for all of us." Jacobi said with a wink.

"Excuse me, but I honestly don't care what works best for the both of you. I can't run away from my life. And if you two were the best bodyguards money can buy, you wouldn't be afraid to let me stay at my house. I mean Kevin Costner didn't make Whitney Houston move out of her house!"

"Didn't Kevin Costner get shot? He took a bullet for her at the end, right?"

Jacobi responded, as he marched up to Angela on the shiny floor of the hallway they were standing on.

She didn't budge, as he was now closer to her face than she'd normally be comfortable with. They had a mini staring contest until Angela gave in. She rolled her eyes, thinking about how much she'd have to pack for a two-week hotel getaway. She ultimately agreed to the plan and told Will she was done working for the night.

She walked to her rental car (as her car was still in the shop from the shooting incident), and Mr. Hicks followed closely behind. He hovered around her keeping his eyes peeled for any sketchy individuals in the parking lot. Jacobi pulled their car around as Mr. Hicks looked under Angela's rental car for any sort of foul play.

Once Mr. Hicks was satisfied, he started the car for Angela and got in the passenger seat. Jacobi followed them to her home, all the while wondering if Angela was going to be this difficult with every proposal they had in mind for her safety.

Jacobi had been in this business for over ten years now, mostly guarding celebrities and people who never needed any serious protection. This particular client seemed like the first person that honestly did need his assistance. He thought about actually taking a bullet for her if the situation called for it. He had been in some serious situations in the past, but had never been shot.

Probably would sting a bit. Nothing I couldn't handle.

Jacobi then pictured Angela's mint-green eyes and how she looked upon him through the glass in her lab. There was something about this woman, something about her gaze that he was a bit mesmerized by. He had told his partner he imagined her differently from all the interviews and articles he had read about her in the last year-and-a-half. He never thought she looked like a doctor, or a scientist, and she especially didn't look like the creator of one of the most influential drugs of his generation. He thought she looked like a woman he'd pick up at a local pub that would have a job at a local pet store.

While Jacobi thought about Angela, she was thinking about Jacobi. Well, when she wasn't answering annoying questions from his partner, Mr. Hicks.

I wonder what Jacobi's first name is? Or, is that his first name?

"What's in this magical love drug anyways? How does it work?" He'd ask.

"It's sort of, complicated. Lot's of scientific jargon you wouldn't understand."

That look in his eyes...I wonder if—

"Yea, I get that. I'm no scientist, Dr. Haven. But, I have a few friends who have taken Pure, and a few of them say it's for the birds. Half of them are still searching. No offense, but I feel like it's almost a ploy for all the *suckers* out there."

"A ploy? No, Mr. Hicks, the drug works. It's always mutual. They'll know without question they are made for each another once they find their person. True...pure...love."

This guy is an idiot. I don't think I'll be able to be around him for—

"Yeah, yeah okay. But I got this friend, Michael, and he's gay, right? He took the drug and 'supposedly' found his true love; this guy named, Billy. And he says it's been great for them two, but Billy brought up having an open relationship. Sure, I get it. Keeps the sex life interesting. But if they really had *true love*, why would Billy even bring up that idea? You know what I'm saying?"

"Relationships are complex and dissimilar for everyone, Mr. Hicks. Pure doesn't change the fact that people want to explore many different preferences for their relationships. Some people can differentiate the variation between sex and love. I'm just happy the LGBTQ community can love whom they are meant to love in this day and age. It's about time."

"Good point. And you know what they say, if you've got the gay's on your side, you're doing something right."

Just shut up. Shut your mouth, you foolish man!

Angela smiled feebly at Mr. Hicks, as they kept driving. Finally, they pulled up into the driveway to her home. Mr. Hicks insisted on walking inside with her, in case there were any intruders waiting for her. Jacobi pulled up behind them and also walked inside after them.

"Well, make yourselves comfortable. I'll be down in a few."

Angela began packing her suitcases. She took her time, not in any rush to leave her home and go to a hotel with these men she had just met. Once she had everything packed, she sat on her bed and looked out the window seeing her beachside view. She shut her eyes imagining someone standing out there looking up at her window, ready to attack her. She took a deep breath and convinced herself this was probably a smart decision.

Jacobi decided to snoop around her hallways to look at the many pictures she had hanging up on her walls.

He saw pictures of Angela celebrating weddings and birthdays with friends. Some pictures were of people that had to be related to her by the color of their mint-green eyes, and familiar smiles. But there was one picture in particular that caught Jacobi's eye. He grabbed it off the wall to examine it closer. It was of Angela and a handsome man—most likely a boyfriend, or ex-boyfriend—and they were hugging in the picture on a beach, as the sun was setting silhouetting their loving embrace.

"I'm ready to go." Angela said, startling Jacobi, causing him to drop the picture of Angela and this nameless man in the picture.

The picture frame hit the floor with a thud and the glass cracked, leaving a shattered spider-web over the picture. Jacobi and Angela both bent down to clean up the mess and Jacobi apologized for dropping the picture. Angela picked it up with great care, disposing of the broken frame. She took a few seconds to stare at the picture in her hands. Jacobi noticed Angela's sad eyes gazing at this sentimental picture.

"Who is this in the picture with you?" Jacobi asked.

"It's…someone from my past."

Angela turned away from Jacobi, opening one of her bags and placed the picture between some of her clothes, zipping the bag back up. She didn't say another word, as she led the two bodyguards out her front door locking it behind her. Jacobi couldn't tell for sure, but it looked as if Angela wiped a tear from her eye in the reflection of the glass door. Knowing this woman for only a couple hours at this point, he could already tell she was a closed off person. She had some walls up, understandably so.

Obviously, Jacobi knew Angela had issues with the nameless man in the picture. She had a past like everyone else. He wasn't going to let that concern him. He was here to protect her. That was his job and he was the best man for it. He thought about taking a bullet for her again, but this time he imagined no pain at all when the bullet hit him.

If you think positively, what could go wrong?

II. Mission Control

Bows was styling her hair in a sixties swirl updo, finishing up the look with two green bows that matched her shapely skintight cocktail dress. Applying the rest of her makeup, she felt the presence of someone behind her, watching her get ready. The men on her team were all scattered inside *Sway*, except for Rocky, who was close by watching Bows get ready from the women's restroom doorframe. *Sway* was closed for the time being, because today was the day; the day the team was to accomplish their current mission.

"Yes?" Bows asked flirtatiously.

She applied her ruby red lipstick slowly and carefully; making sure Rocky was still watching her in the mirror.

"Look at that fine ass. Get over here."

"Go find something else to do…your good-looking face is distracting me."

Bows smiled sweetly, looking in the mirror watching Rocky smile back at her in the reflection. Leaving her be, Rocky walked down the hall and into the main lounge where the stage was set up. Boulder was waiting for his brother on the stage and started dealing each of them a handful of cards. He was ready to gamble and take money from Rocky.

Worm and Ace were at the bar, both smoking cigarettes and conversing. Worm had two laptops in front of him, fiddling away at the keyboards, as fast as his fingers could type. His red mohawk was now tipped with a vibrant blue.

"What are you doing?" Ace asked, watching his comrade type a mile a minute.

"I'm creating computer viruses and sending them to my ex-girlfriend."

"And, why are you doing this?"

"Because she's a cheating bitch."

Ace didn't ask any more questions about the matter. He knew Worm had some really bad luck with the ladies recently and he didn't want to get him going on one of his "woman-hating" rants.

"Not only am I sending her countless viruses, I'm also closing her bank accounts and finding the most grotesque pornography I can, so I can send the links to her coworkers from her email address."

"Doesn't Liz work at a preschool?"

"Don't say her garbage name. No one cheats on me and gets away with it!"

"Damn. Remind me to never get on your bad side."

Ace took the last drag from his cigarette, still craving another. He had quite the smoking habit, especially after he took it up again after what happened with his relationship with Bows.

"You know what, Ace? I'm glad we're doing this mission today. This woman, Dr. Haven, deserves what's coming to her. I should never have taken that stupid drug. Pure has messed up too many lives. This world was such a better place when everyone wasn't looking for that spark that Pure supposedly ignites."

"Even before Pure, people were looking for the spark, man. Did you think you had the spark with Liz?"

"Ah, shit, no. I mean, maybe. But that's the whole point of Pure, right? It isn't a *maybe*. It works, without a doubt, and your entire being knows this person is right for you. I guess if I think about it, when our eyes locked when we first met, I didn't feel it."

"So how can you blame Dr. Haven? You knew what you were getting yourself into. Everyone who took it knew...including me."

Ace desperately wanted to make himself a drink, but recognized he couldn't. Snipers had to have extreme focus and alcohol wasn't a good strategic notion before the mission.

"Yea, and see how well that worked out for you and Bows?"

Worm had a horrible habit of saying things he shouldn't have said in the first place.

"I'm an asshole, Ace. I'm sorry, buddy. I'm just sick of the search. It's a constant let-down with every woman I make eye contact with."

Watching Worm send his ex-girlfriend the viruses, Ace couldn't help but snicker.

"I want to go back to the simpler days. It wasn't nearly as depressing. Love doesn't have to be a definite thing. It should be reckless and mysterious. Keeping you on your toes. I don't know about you, but I'm definitely ready to let this doctor have what's coming to her."

"Would you be able to pull the trigger on this one?" Ace asked, knowing Worm was a complete softie even if he did talk a big game.

"My fingers belong on the keyboards and your fingers belong on the guns. I wouldn't want to mess up the system we have that works so well for the team."

Ace chuckled to himself again hearing Worm's excuse. He had enough of this conversation and decided he needed some alone time to reflect on his thoughts. A good amount of alone time before each mission was always beneficial for his peace of mind. It took a lot of high-focused energy to be a sniper. Sometimes, he'd be sitting in an enclosed space for days waiting for the right moment to pull the trigger.

This particular mission wouldn't take too long with his team working as one; they'd get this mission done within a matter of hours. Right as he walked outside *Sway*'s front doors, he received a text from his boss, Duke.

COME TO MY OFFICE ASAP.

This should be good...

Ace made his way back into *Sway* and walked past Worm, listening to his maniacal laughing, typing away at his multiple computers.

Issues...

He then walked past the stage; viewing Boulder and Rocky play cards. Boulder had a stack of cash next to him and Rocky looked pissed.

Ha, ha, douchebag...

Ace smirked at Rocky like a wise guy and Rocky held up his middle finger. Walking towards Duke's office, Ace wondered why Duke needed to see him. As he pondered this, Bows came out of the women's bathroom all dolled up, looking a bit startled to see her ex-boyfriend standing right outside the door.

"Ace, damn it, you scared me. Where's Rocky?"

"What do I look like, his keeper?"

"Real mature." She said, walking away swinging her tiny hips back and forth, down the hallway towards the main lounge.

Nice job, Ace.

Finally reaching Duke's office, Ace took a deep breath and knocked on his door. He didn't know why he was nervous to meet with Duke; but he didn't like the feeling he had in the pit of his stomach.

"Come in, Ace." Duke shouted from inside his office.

Ace opened the door and walked in taking a seat at Duke's desk.

"You wanted to see me?"

"Yes, I wanted to make some changes with this mission. I understand you all work well with one another as is, but I've decided for this particular mission I'd like you to be the mission leader."

Ace was taken aback by what Duke had suggested, or rather, ordered, since he was the head honcho of the team. Ace had only been mission leader on a few missions that didn't involve using his sniper rifle. But this mission involved the use of his skills, so he was quite confused by this decision.

"But sir, Rocky always leads the missions when I'm behind the scope. I don't understand why you'd like me to lead while I'll be focusing on the target?"

"That's exactly why you need to lead this mission. You'll be at the highest vantage point. You'll be seeing more than Rocky and everyone else on the team. I need this mission to go as smoothly as possible and although Rocky has never let me down before, he can be quite sloppy with his methods. He can be too impulsive. You have great control and careful execution while you lead missions. That's what I need for this particular case."

"He won't like it. He'll feel like I'm taking his position."

"Well, if he has a problem with it, he can take it up with me. And besides, sometimes people take things that don't outright belong to them."

Duke nudged Ace's arm to drive the point home. Of course Ace knew he was referring to Rocky dating (and now moving in with) Bows after their break-up.

Why can't everyone just let that go? Taking Pure fucked everything up for us.

Duke shook Ace's hand and led him out of his office. Ace had been requested to inform Rocky of the mission leader modification. From this moment on, his fellow team members had an hour before getting into place.

Duke had eyes everywhere, and he rarely ever let on how he knew where his targets would be for the team's missions. He had many knowledgeable informants that Ace, and the other team members, weren't privileged to know about. Ace didn't think about this much. He had one job and that was to follow Duke's orders.

That's how he made his livelihood. That's how he stayed safe as an undercover bartender. That's how he lived his life, even if he occasionally wondered what it'd be like to be a decent person that didn't assassinate people for a living.

Then again, he didn't think about this much.

Rocky had just lost all his money to his brother, once again. Being the troublemaker he always was, Ace thought this was the perfect opportunity to let Rocky know he was going to take his position as mission leader. The look on Rocky's face was priceless when Ace gave him the bad news. And as Rocky made his way to the front doors of *Sway*, Ace heard him punch the lounge wall slamming open the front doors to light up a joint.

A hazy cloud of white smoke lingered in the air, with the strong scent of some fresh marijuana. Ace also made his way out the front doors of *Sway* and caught a strong whiff of it. He tiptoed behind Rocky and tapped him on the shoulder.

Rocky scoffed. "What do you want?"

"As mission leader, I want your head in the game, so no more of this."

"It helps me focus."

Ace grabbed the joint from Rocky's lips and threw it on the pavement. With a giant grin on his face, Ace casually walked back inside *Sway*. He noticed Bows leaning against the bar with her arms folded, having just witnessed the interaction between her ex-boyfriend and her current boyfriend. She discerned Rocky was pissed by the way he kicked *Sway*'s red velvet rope over.

Still smiling, Ace shouted, "Get ready! We're out in five flat." Turning towards Bows, he whispered, "Your boy toy has quite an anger problem."

Bows turned away from Ace and stomped off towards Boulder who was still counting his earnings from his brother. Worm was now sobbing at the bar saying, "What have I done?"

He was regretting sending the computer viruses to his ex-girlfriend. But, Ace was in the happiest of moods. He was actually excited about this mission, especially the part where he would be ordering Rocky around. He looked down at his phone and there was another text from Duke.

DON'T LET ME DOWN.

Ace kept on smiling, knowing he had this mission in the bag. He knew the mission was going to be a piece of cake, being an overconfident type of person he aimed to be. After all, he was the leader now and when he was in control, things always turned out better than expected.

What could go wrong?

CHAPTER 3

UNDER CONTROL

I. A Plan is Starting to Appear

Angela rubbed her tired eyes. The obnoxious sounds of Mr. Hicks' snoring kept her and Jacobi tossing and turning most of the night.

Angela was the first to wake up after finally falling asleep for a stretch of hours and stood next to the hotel suite window beside her bed. The Watermark Hotel was nothing short of a high-class hotel with all the amenities one could ever want. Angela opened the curtains and stared off into the distance watching the ocean's beautiful blues and greens splash around for miles. Pressing her cold hand against the warm window, she longed for a quick swim.

With her two bodyguards hovering around her, Angela began to feel like a prisoner. She walked into the main room of the luxury suite to find Jacobi putting a white undershirt on, rubbing the eye snot out of his sleepy eyes.

"And how'd you sleep, Dr. Haven?"

"Delightfully. Thanks to the soothing sounds Mr. Hicks was making through his nostrils all night."

"Tell me about it. I threw every pillow I had at him to get him to simmer down, but he was dead to the world."

"One of my bodyguards is a heavy sleeper; that's comforting."

Angela made her way over to the kitchen area and began to make some hot tea to wake herself up. Jacobi hit the floor and began his morning ritual of doing 100 pushups. Angela couldn't help but glance over in his direction, as Jacobi had quite a muscular body. He abruptly turned his head towards Angela and caught her checking him out. Of course, Angela averted her eyes straightaway, examining the kitchen countertop. Jacobi just smiled and continued his routine.

"I was thinking of going for a swim this morning. I love being in the ocean, it just makes me feel—"

"Sorry, but that's not going to happen today, Dr. Haven." Jacobi interrupted.

Standing up again, Jacobi knew he wouldn't be able to finish the rest of his morning pushups ritual if he'd have to get into it with Dr. Haven.

"First of all, call me Angela. Second of all, you can't tell me what to do. You were hired to protect me and I'm allowing that…but only from the sandy shore. I apologize if you get a bit hot out there in your suit, but every job comes with unfortunate aspects."

"Being out in the general public, when you've already been attacked, isn't the smartest idea right now. I can draw a bath for you, if you'd like?" Jacobi asked, being completely serious about his suggestion.

Angela wasn't pleased with his condescending tone. "I don't want to lay in a bathtub. I want to swim in the ocean. I get it; my life sucks right now. I can't do a lot of the things I did before I created Pure, but I will *not* stop living the life I want for myself. Swimming in the ocean relaxes me. It's something I need. And I need it today."

Mr. Hicks woke up abruptly and sat up from the couch he was sleeping on. He decided to chime in without even opening his eyes.

"No, he's right, Dr. Haven. We can't allow it. I'm sorry—"

"Oh, now you're up! And like I told your bullheaded partner, call me Angela!"

Angela obviously wasn't going to get her way with these two, so she poured herself a cup of tea and stormed off to her room, slamming the door behind her.

"Someone's cranky this morning." Mr. Hicks muttered, stretching his arms above his head with a loud yawn.

Jacobi just smirked and said, "I've got her under control."

At that very second, Angela was slipping on her new light blue bikini, forging a plan of escape from her overbearing bodyguards.

II. In the Driver's Seat

"I think I'm going to throw up," Bows declared, holding her hand over her mouth. With her other hand, she squeezed Rocky's arm in the backseat of Duke's blacked-out van. "You suck at driving, Worm!"

"That's because he's wiping the stream of tears from his crying eyes." Ace shouted in an irritated manner.

Being the mission leader seemed to be a stress for Ace and the mission itself hadn't even started yet. He wasn't comfortable with his team being distracted, especially with emotional relationship issues.

"Piss off! All of you! I'm just going through a lot at the moment!" Worm shouted back, blowing his nose into his linen handkerchief.

Ace rolled down the passenger side window and exhaled loudly. "Get it together, Worm!"

The van was cramped with the teams' weapons and high-tech computer systems. Everyone felt nauseous from Worm's topsy-turvy driving. Ace immediately regretted his decision to designate Worm the driver, all for the sake of *keeping his mind off things.*

"Lizzy broke my heart. I can't even think about her with another man. It's driving me crazy! I could kill that two-timing slut!"

Another car cut in front of the van and Worm suddenly slammed on the brakes, causing his snotty handkerchief to fly across the dashboard and onto Ace's lap. This, of course, enraged Ace to no end, and so he threw the handkerchief out the window.

"Hey! That was given to me as a Christmas present from Lizzy!"

"Pull over, damn it!"

Ace had apparently had enough of Worm's antics and awful driving. Worm pulled over and shut off the engine. Ace took the keys out of the ignition and handed them to Boulder.

"You're driving."

"If you insist, but I was drinking this morning." Boulder grumbled.

Ace grabbed the keys out of Boulder's hand and tossed them to Rocky.

"You're driving."

"I don't have a license." Rocky said, glaring at Ace.

Bows spoke up and asked, "Why don't you have a license, babe?"

"It expired and I never went to renew it. Remember? The day I was supposed to go, you wouldn't let us get out of bed."

Ace's blood pressure was skyrocketing at this point. "Bows, you're driving!"

"Don't speak to me like that!"

"I'm the mission leader! It's your job to follow my orders!" Ace argued back.

Bows climbed up front and switched spots with Worm. "You don't have to be an ass about it."

"I don't have time for this bullshit. I'll drive. Switch spots with me, Bows." Ace unbuckled his seat belt and opened the passenger side door and stepped outside. It was a steamy 95 degrees out and climbing this morning. Wiping the sweat off his brow, Ace stomped towards the driver's side of the van as Bows sat calmly filing her nails in the passenger seat.

This is going to be a damn disaster if we don't get our shit together.

At that thought, Ace looked into the distance and saw a police car driving down the road. It looked as though the police officer was slowing down as he drove closer, but then he continued on past the van. Ace grabbed the gold cross on his necklace and squeezed it, giving the man upstairs a quick head nod.

Thank you, God...that's the last thing we needed right now.

As if the policeman could sense Ace's worriment, the police car screeched to a halt, turned around and pulled up next to the van. Worm was now sitting in the passenger seat, as Ace lit up a cigarette outside the van. The police officer had his window down and stuck his head out of the window slightly.

"You havin' some car trouble?" The officer asked in a southern accent.

Ace didn't panic, even though he knew if the officer were to check inside the van, they'd have a murdered officer on their hands.

"No, Officer. We're just switching drivers. Taking a long road trip here." Ace lied.

The Officer stepped out of his vehicle and walked the length of the van examining it with shiny sunglasses over his eyes. Ace couldn't tell if he was sweating from the heat, or the nerves he was experiencing from this lousy bad luck.

"Can I see your license and registration, mister?" The police officer asked, as Rocky, Worm and Boulder crouched in the back of the van, hands on their guns and ready for any trouble this officer might bring.

"Absolutely, sir."

Ace opened the front door of the van and just like a professional, Bows had already fixed her cleavage so the officer could get a good look at her handing Ace the registration papers. She winked at the officer and smiled. He, of course, tipped his hat to her.

While Ace handed the Officer his license and registration, he wanted to have a bit of fun in this scenario.

"My girlfriend and I are on our way to her mother's house. Take *all* the time you need, Officer." Ace said with a light snicker, as the officer chuckled at his joke.

The officer took a look into the van and made eye contact with Bows again. She was stretching her arms above her head, pushing her chest out ever so slightly.

No more than a few seconds later, he handed Ace's license back to him, while trying to get a few coy looks at Bows while he could.

"You're a lucky man. Try to enjoy yourselves today. Drive safe now, ya here?"

The police officer sped off and Ace wiped the sweat off his forehead, again, taking a deep breath of fresh air before shutting the door.

"Yea…I still got it." Bows said with a pat on her back.

"Now that everything's under control, let's get a move on. We're already behind schedule." Ace said, pulling back onto the street and driving down the road with a clear focused mind, ready for the mission ahead. He had hoped his bad luck would end there.

III. Sound the Alarm

Peeking out her door, Angela could see a freshly showered Jacobi, wrapped up in a white hotel towel around his trim waist. She couldn't help but take a few seconds to examine his shredded body. The droplets of water cascading down his rippling abs were distracting her from visualizing her goal, which was getting out of the hotel room without her bodyguards suspecting she had even left. She heard Mr. Hicks coughing up a lung in the kitchen area of the hotel suite and thought of the perfect opportunity to get him out of the room.

Putting on a pair of blue jean cut-offs and a pink spaghetti strap tank top over her bathing suit, Angela decided to make her move. She knew she'd have to be sneaky and clever about the way she was going to have to handle this get-away situation. Walking out of her room she passed the bathroom (where Jacobi was getting dressed), and tiptoed into the kitchen as fast as she could.

"Sounds like you have a pretty bad cough there, Mr. Hicks."

Clearing his throat, he replied, "Oh, it's nothing to be concerned about. I've had this cold for over a week now. It's unpleasant, but I'll be as healthy as a horse in no time. Unless you have a magical elixir for me?"

"I *am* a doctor. I know some serious pills that can knock that cold out of your system by the end of the day. Here you go," Angela handed Mr. Hicks a piece of paper with the names of some strong medications written down upon it.

"There's a pharmacy down the block from this hotel. I saw it as we drove in. I'd feel safer having both my bodyguards as healthy as they can be."

"I do feel like shit in a hand basket right now, excuse my language. You make a good point; I should be in the best health I can be…for you. I'll go down there," Mr. Hicks exclaimed. "Just as soon as Jacobi gets out of the bathroom and can keep an eye on you."

Damn! He's on to me.

"Sounds like a plan, Mr. Hicks."

Angela turned her back to Mr. Hicks, quickly planning how she'd distract Jacobi for enough time to get out of this prison for a daytime dip in the ocean. Angela collapsed on the couch and let out an exasperated sigh of frustration. She thought about her life before she had invented Pure and wished she could go back to those days. Everything was simpler. She could come and go as she pleased without the threat of crazy people trying to shoot her.

Then again, she thought of all the people she had brought together from the discovery of Pure. Surely, the countless thousands of couples who found one another owed her a bit of their happiness.

How is it my fault these other crazy people haven't found their own true loves? It's so easy to blame others when you aren't truly happy with your own life.

Jacobi came out of the bathroom wearing a long sleeved white dress shirt, with the sleeves rolled up, dark grey dress pants and navy blue socks.

"Don't judge me, but there's no way in hell I'm wearing a jacket and tie today. It's disgustingly hot out there." He said, sitting on the couch next to Angela. Slipping his dress shoes on and tying them tight, he looked like he was posing as a Greek statue.

Jacobi stood up and walked to the kitchen, where Mr. Hicks was eating what smelled like an English muffin covered in peanut butter. He was, of course, wearing his suit jacket and a tie.

"If you're all dressed for the day, I'm going to make a short errand to the pharmacy. Angela was lovely enough to write down some medication for this awful cold. I should be back in half an hour."

"Pick me up an energy drink, please?" Jacobi asked.

"I will not. I won't be enabling that terrible addiction of yours. And you, Dr. Hav—uh, Angela, please behave yourself and listen to Jacobi."

"Of course, Mr. Hicks." Angela said, with the necessary smile on her face.

Mr. Hicks grabbed his wallet and gun from the kitchen counter, and walked out of the hotel room clearing his congested throat, shutting the door behind him.

One down...

"So what's on the agenda for you today, Jacobi?" Angela asked, sidestepping into her room. She wanted to seem curious, but not overly pushy.

"Well, that's pretty much up to you."

"If it's up to me, we're off to the beach."

"We went over this. It's not safe to be out in the public at this time. There's an Olympic sized pool on the fourth floor with a nice gym. There's a four-star restaurant and even a movie theater in this hotel. Trust me, you won't be bored while we're here. You just have to compromise a bit. You understand why you can't be out in the open, right?"

Yes, I understand...that you talk to me like I'm a child.

"Of course. You're just protecting me. I get it. Well, in that case, I'm off to the pool." Angela said, slipping her sandals on.

Jacobi went to the closet and grabbed a towel for her, opening the door of the hotel room suite for her.

"After you..."

"What are you doing?" Angela asked.

"What does it look like I'm doing? I'm accompanying you to the pool."

"I don't need a babysitter, Jacobi. I think I can handle going to the pool without being attacked, but thank you for your concern. You don't have to be by my side 24/7."

"Actually, I do. Dr. Rayne is paying us good money to do just that. Besides, it's not like I don't trust you, but...well, that's exactly what it is. I don't trust you. If I let you out of my sight, we both know you'd head directly to the beach. I'm not letting that happen."

I thought the jock types were supposed to be dumb.

"Fine, let's go to the pool...together. If that's the only way I can get my swim on, then so be it."

Jacobi smiled and grabbed Angela's beach bag for her, leading her to the door, never wiping the smirk from his face. The elevator ride down was a quiet one, allowing Angela to form her plan into existence. She grabbed her beach bag from Jacobi's hand as the elevator door opened. They walked side-by-side down the hotel hallway to the spa area of the hotel--which is where the indoor pool was also located—and it was completely empty. The pool area was also empty, as all the guests were most likely at the beach since it was such a beautiful day outside. Jacobi slunk into a poolside chair, expecting Angela to stop walking, but she was clearly heading towards the women's locker room first.

"Don't you already have your bathing suit on?" He asked accusatorily.

"Yes, but I still have to freshen up, if that's all right with you?" Angela was gripping the straps of her beach bag tightly hoping Jacobi would give her the time she needed to escape from the hotel.

Jacobi squinted his eyes at Angela. He was trying to read her face, trying to decipher if he could trust her enough to let her out of his sight for a short amount of time.

"You've got less than five minutes. Otherwise, I'm storming in there without any hesitation."

"Yes, sir." Angela said, giving him a salute with her right hand.

Once she was inside, she ran towards the opposite side of the locker room and knew at once what her next move had to be. It was risky, but at this point, she was backed into a corner.

Just pull it, Angela. You don't have any other choice!

Angela had never pulled a fire alarm in her life. She never thought she'd be in the situation to pull one, so she was extremely nervous about actually going through with it, but she recited the quote she lived by anytime she needed to get some courage:

"Fortune favors the brave..."

It worked every time. Angela put her fingers on the lever and pressed down, causing the alarm to sound off. Without a second's delay, Jacobi knew what Angela had done. Running from his chair to the women's locker room, he opened the door making his way through the maze of lockers leading him to the back row of the locker room, where he saw the exit door cracked open.

Damn her!

Jacobi sprinted out the exit door and ran around to the back of the hotel where he knew Angela was headed. The beach was filled with countless people enjoying the sun's rays.

After the confusion of the fire alarm, the hotel was now emptying quickly. There could be no way of singling out Angela through the enormous crowds of people. But it didn't stop Jacobi from trying.

Jogging on the sandy beach barefoot (since he didn't have time to put his dress shoes back on in the pool area), Jacobi made his way through the many beach towels with half naked sunbather's tanning. As he passed by a group of young women tanning, he heard one of them give him a flirtatious whistle.

"Look at that Michael B. Jordan brother in the suit…fine as hell…"

He tried to spot Angela through the crowds of people searching person by person. But the bright sun was bouncing off the glimmering ocean waves into his light brown eyes and he couldn't make Angela's figure out on the beach, or in the water. He called Mr. Hicks immediately and told him about the situation at hand. Of course, Mr. Hicks started yelling uncontrollably at Jacobi's stupidity for letting Angela get away.

"We treated her like a child, Hicks. She wasn't our prisoner!" Jacobi shouted back.

He told Mr. Hicks to meet him on the beach and hopefully two pairs of eyes could spot their missing client faster than one pair. Mr. Hicks told

Jacobi he'd be right there, but this didn't comfort Jacobi. Somewhere out there, Angela was by herself. Defenseless. Alone. Unprotected.

You'll find her. She's going to be fine...

At least that's what he kept telling himself to make the sickening feeling in the pit of his stomach subside. But alas, it wasn't working...

CHAPTER 4

FEELING BETTER

I. Hot as Hell

Ace and his crew arrived at the Church of St. Anthony. This church was shut down and abandoned due to financial reasons, but it was never torn down because of its historical relevance to the small town of Santa Margarita. Ace and his crew were stationed at this location since it was in close proximity to the Watermark Hotel—being directly across the street.

And furthermore, there was an ideal bell tower for Ace to be posted in. The tower was the highest point in the city and Ace would be able to see the entire front entrance of the hotel, as well as the beach beyond it. With his crew's help, he'd have Dr. Haven in his gun's sight in no time.

Boulder had his shirt off due to the intense heat, and also because he was passing time jumping rope at one of the alters of the church. Sweat dripped down his chest and muscular back, while he gazed at the masterful artwork on the ceilings and the many colors of the stained-glass windows. Being a simple man, the beauty of this art was lost on Boulder. However, he did appreciate the hard work and time that must have gone into the labor.

At the same time, Bows was appreciating her own beauty, making sure her complexion was flawless using just the right shades of purple eye shadow. She noticed Rocky was smiling at her from a distance and thought about how truly happy she was to have found her one true love. She was ready for this mission to be over. All she wanted was some alone time away from the crew and to be with Rocky on some remote island.

Right before she closed her compact mirror, she made eye contact with Ace, who was cleaning his sniper rifle in the corner of the church. She tried not to think about how awful it must be for him to see her with Rocky. They had been lovers once upon a time, and had even discussed their future as a couple.

> It's ironic that we're about to kill the woman who was
> responsible for bringing Rocky and I together. It's a bit wicked
> of us, but oh well. Hopefully this will give Ace some closure
> about us, once he pulls the trigger.

Concentrating on cleaning the singular components of his gun and making sure every piece of the deadly weapon was intact, Ace didn't have time to contemplate how he felt about assassinating the woman who invented the love drug that ruined his relationship with Bows. He had a mission to complete, and that's what he focused on.

Out of the corner of his eye, Ace viewed Bows getting all dolled up, fanning herself with a small handheld fan. He was still captivated by her beauty even if he knew she would never be his again. She caught him looking at her backside multiple times. She decided to ignore it and stroll over to Rocky, taking a seat on his lap.

"Babe, it's too hot to sit on my lap right now."

Bows just scoffed at her boyfriend as she walked away from him towards Worm. Worm was sitting a few pews down, with a laptop on his lap and two tablets on either side of him. He was in a complete hacking zone, typing codes and numerical combinations that Bows couldn't even begin to comprehend.

"How's it coming along, Wormy?" she asked, still fanning herself so her makeup wouldn't smear.

"Shh…" Worm whispered continuing his furious typing.

So, again, Bows rolled her eyes and walked to the corner of the church standing before Ace, as he continued to inspect, polish and clean all the parts of his sniper rifle.

"Next time we rendezvous at an old abandoned church, can you make sure it has air conditioning?" She asked, continuing to fan her face.

"Wow, you know what the word 'rendezvous' means? Who are you and what have you done with Bows?"

"You're not even remotely funny, Ace. You know I hate when people dismiss my intelligence because of my beauty."

Ace was looking into the scope of his rifle checking the wind resistance kilometers, trying to keep a straight face. He knew his ex-girlfriend was insecure about anything that didn't concern her beautiful looks and he played into that as much as he could. Ignoring her now, Ace knew this would infuriate her even more, not giving her the satisfaction of responding.

Spinning in a circle with her arms out like a helicopter, Bows asked, "I'm so bored. When do we get to have fun?"

At times, she could be so juvenile; but even at those moments, she was captivating to watch.

"I'm about done here," Ace whispered under his breath, and then raised his voice bellowing, "Worm! How's it coming along in there?"

"All systems are a-go here, Captain! Just a matter of minutes!" Worm shouted back.

Worm was delegated the duty of finding the room Dr. Haven was staying in. Of course, it wasn't exactly an easy task being that the room wasn't listed under her name. But Worm could hack anything. He hacked into the Watermark's computer system and ruled out any rooms that didn't fit the parameters Duke had briefed the crew about.

The crew was given specific information about Angela Haven and they knew she was staying at the Watermark Hotel with two bodyguards the prior night. Worm ruled out rooms that were occupied for longer than a day as well as one-room suites. With that alone, he eliminated majority of the rooms and was left with 28 rooms that could be Dr. Haven's.

While Worm continued to narrow down which room was hers, Ace went over the plan with Bows, Rocky and Boulder once more before giving them each an earpiece communication device that would act as a walkie-talkie and the go-ahead to disperse.

Of course, Rocky had a few "suggestions" of his own, but Ace shot them down without taking the time to really listen. Ace could almost hear Rocky's teeth grinding in frustration. Rocky took the lead, being the first to walk outside the church. Boulder and Bows followed quickly thereafter walking out the front doors and across the street.

Ace locked the doors behind them, carrying his gun case with one hand, while the other held onto his lucky gold cross that hung around his neck. He had it on every mission, except for one, in which he suffered a nasty lower back injury—caused by getting thrown into a glass table by his intended target. If it wasn't for Boulder coming to his aid, he might've bled to death. Since that incident, Ace always made sure to wear his lucky cross. He didn't think of himself as a superstitious person, but during his missions, he didn't take any chances. He usually hid the necklace under his shirt, for he was sick of his crew giving him antagonisms about his "beliefs."

While Bows and Ace were still together, she had asked him about his religious views. She wanted to know about his cross in particular.

"Why do you even bother wearing that silly necklace? I mean, you assassinate people for a living, for Christ's sake."

Ace thought it over, and simply replied, "Forgiveness, Bows. It's a powerful notion."

Bows laughed in his face and replied, "If that's what you need to tell yourself to sleep at night..."

That was a long time ago, but of course, Ace's crew still didn't respect his religious beliefs—especially knowing he had the highest body count out of the entire crew, thus far.

Worm was getting closer to narrowing down the search for Dr. Haven's room with only 11 options left. Making sure his earpiece communication device was working properly, Ace wished him luck. Worm wished him luck as well, for Ace had the more challenging task of this mission.

The rest of the crew all responded back on their earpieces within seconds. Everyone was on the same channel, as they were now headed towards the Watermark Hotel's entrance. However, the hotel manager wasn't letting anyone in since the fire alarm was still going off.

"Seven rooms to go, Captain." Worm announced.

Bows pressed her earpiece and told the team why there was a standstill happening at the hotel, while Ace gave the order to wait outside since they had no choice in the matter anyways.

Making his way towards the back hallway of the church where the spiral staircase was located, Ace took a deep breath and started climbing the stairs one by one. He listened to the creaking wood stairs groan and breathe. His palms were quite sweaty and the gun case was slipping from his callused grip. He thought it must be from the extreme heat, but then he noticed his heartbeat racing.

Confident and focused: those were usually the words to describe Ace's mentality on missions, but at this moment, he was clearly overly nervous and overwhelmed. He couldn't place why exactly; as he had been doing this for years and this wasn't even the first time he was mission leader.

Halfway up the spiral staircase, he had to grab the railing beside him, for fear he would fall backwards. Something wasn't right. He wasn't physically and mentally in the right state for this mission, but he knew he had to get focused quickly. Shaky hands and an unfocused mind was a sniper's worst enemy.

Just breathe, Ace. Breathe…

One step at a time, Ace made his way up the stairs, which seemed to be endless, to the very top of the church tower. And with each stair, the heat seemed to engulf his lungs, making Ace gasp for clean air in the dusty staircase. He attempted to pray, holding onto his gold cross as he spoke to whoever was listening in the sky above. At first he felt a bit silly praying right before he was about to assassinate an innocent person, but then he convinced himself that everything happens for a reason; and the reason his team was supposed to terminate this woman was because she destroyed people's lives.

She's no saint. I'm doing the world a favor by getting rid of her.

Meanwhile, outside the Watermark Hotel, Rocky and Boulder stood behind a very important-looking Bows. She was speaking to an employee of the hotel with her hands on her hips and giant sunglasses over her eyes.

"How much longer is this going to take?" Bows interrogated.

The hotel employee retorted, "As soon as we make sure there aren't any fire hazards present, we will let everyone back inside."

"We haven't even checked in, yet." Bows said.

"Well, don't hold this against us. This is an unusual circumstance. Please, enjoy your stay here at the Watermark."

"Oh, I'm sure we'll have a *killer* time!" Bows said, with a grin on her face.

Boulder rolled his eyes at Bow's obvious pun. He wasn't too fond of his brother's girlfriend, thinking she thought too much of herself most of the time, but his brother was happy with her so he tolerated her as best he could.

After what seemed like forever, Ace reached the top of the staircase and budged the tower door open. Stepping inside, Ace looked upon a small octagon-shaped room, with large windows on each side, letting the bright sunlight streak in. Ace took a breath of fresh air and began to feel much better.

His shakiness was subsiding and his heartbeat was slowing down to a proper relaxed state. He loosened his grip on the steel gun case, setting it down on the wooden floor. He looked down upon the Watermark Hotel and realized this tower was the ultimate position to assassinate Dr. Haven from. The next phase was to confirm with the rest of his crew that he was now in his preparation stage.

The sweat dripping down his face was a bit distracting while he was placing the separate pieces of his weapon together. Once the sniper rifle was all composed, loaded, and aimed at the hotel entrance, Ace laid flat on his stomach and was now in 'set to kill' position. It was a waiting game at this point. It was now time for the rest of his crew to do their jobs, so he could have a clear shot at Dr. Haven.

He looked into the gun sight and knew with perfect clarity—he was ready...

II. Under the Sea

There were crowds of guests filing out of the hotel and onto the beach like a mass of ants swarming around an anthill. The fire alarm could be heard from the edge of the beach, where Angela was now standing with both of her feet in the sparkling ocean water. She didn't wipe the sweat droplets from her forehead or upper lip, knowing she would be swimming under the water soon enough. Angela turned her head back to the beach to look at the beach bag she had placed just a few yards away from her.

She had already taken her cut-offs and pink spaghetti-strapped tank top and put them into the beach bag with her phone, purse, and sunscreen. Hearing the fire alarm continue to drone on, she couldn't believe she had been such a rebel. Angela also couldn't predict how much time she had to enjoy the water before her pesky bodyguards would tackle her and carry her over their shoulders back to her prison cell. She tried to spot Jacobi or Mr. Hicks, but with all the commotion happening on the beach, she couldn't spot either of them through the crowd. The bright sun wasn't helping her see clearly, but it felt wonderful on her pale skin. Since she was inside most days, she didn't have a great base tan.

With a smile on her face, Angela briskly stepped into the waves, which slapped her shins and splashed her thighs with a refreshing mist. Tilting her head back, she took the hair tie out of her hair and put it around her wrist feeling her golden locks blow in the light breeze that was coming off the ocean. When she was waist high in the water, she whirled around looking back to the sandy shore, feeling as though she was being watched, but still couldn't make out Jacobi or Mr. Hicks.

What a mess you've caused...you might as well enjoy this while you can.

Diving into a massive wave, Angela felt the chilly water engulf her petite body. Her mind went back to the days when she was just a little girl, daydreaming about being a mermaid. She didn't have a care in the world back then. Those were the days she had all her walls down and was so willing to let people in. She didn't have to protect herself from untrue stories about her in the paparazzi or get hurt from the men who pursued her for her newfound money.

Angela let go all of her stress and anxiety while she was under the water. Continuing to swim her heart out, she didn't think about her current situation. She just enjoyed the time she had made for herself in the ocean's abyss. Stretching her body out, she felt the pull of the currents choose where her body drifted. Never once did she realize how close she was to death's door. But for the time being, she was perfectly content.

III. Distraction

Jacobi was frantically searching the beach and the open ocean for any hint of Angela's athletic figure, but there was no sign of her. In all actuality, he thought she might not have come to the beach at all. Or maybe she did—and an outraged maniac had already attacked her, drowning her in the ocean. Thinking about all the possible scenarios, Jacobi realized how concerned he was for Angela. He was hired to protect her and even though she tricked him to get away, he was still responsible for her well-being.

Mr. Hicks was calling Jacobi's cell phone from the hotel parking lot, but the signal wasn't strong enough, resulting in one dropped call after another. Frustrated about his cell phone service, Mr. Hicks decided to search for Angela on his own. The medicine Dr. Haven had recommended already seemed to be helping his cough calm down. He popped in a cough drop while he untied his dress shoes and stripped his socks off throwing them into the car passenger seat. If there was one thing Mr. Hicks hated, it was the feel of sand under his feet—especially with shoes on.

Trudging through the sand with a scowl on his aged face, Mr. Hicks cursed himself for forgetting his sunglasses in the hotel suite. He couldn't see a damned thing with the sunlight blinding his vulnerable squinty eyes.

I'm getting too old for this shit.

Hearing the fire alarm finally shut off from the hotel, Mr. Hicks made his way through the crowds of hotel guests. They were all gathered together in between the hotel parking lot and the beach. At this point, the hotel managers were outside informing the guests of the false alarm, letting everyone know it was safe to reenter the hotel. Passing by a woman and two large men through this crowd, Mr. Hicks wondered what type of grown woman still wore bows in her hair.

As more and more guests scurried back inside the air-conditioned hotel, Mr. Hicks tried to call Jacobi once more. He hung up as soon as he dialed his number because he saw his partner frantically maneuvering along the shore with his hand above his eyes, trying to search for Angela.

"Jacobi!" Mr. Hicks shouted in his direction.

Jacobi spun around and saw his partner walking towards him. He was relieved, knowing two pairs of eyes were better than one.

Back at the church, Worm was informing the crew he had the search narrowed down to two rooms. And they were both on the executive floor of the Watermark Hotel.

Bows and Rocky were distracted with their spontaneous make out session on the beach, while Boulder pressed his earpiece and informed the team the hotel was now allowing guests back inside. Rocky and Bows quickly composed themselves and decided it was time to get down to business. They walked inside with the other guests, and after some clever persuasion, Bows used her fake credit card and driver's license to book a room on the executive floor. The bellhop escorted the three miscreants to the elevators. The young bellhop attempted to show them to their room, but Boulder told him to get lost without tipping him a dime.

Once inside their room, Bows looked at her reflection in the mirror and lifted her knee-high dress to her upper-thigh, revealing a sharp six-inch blade tucked beneath her thin leather and laced garter. This was her weapon of choice, as she wasn't a fan of guns. She wasn't particularly a fan of any weapon usually, as the men in her crew handled most of the dirty work. Nevertheless, Bows wasn't a helpless damsel who was just a pretty face; she was trained for hand-to-hand combat and basic weaponry. If it came down to a fight to the death, she was confident she could hold her own with a short blade. Even the smallest cuts could be deadly if she severed the right vein.

Rocky and his older brother were expert fighters who could assassinate any target with the use of their strong hands, but some of the times, their targets weren't in hand-to-hand distance and they needed to be prepared to use their guns. Rocky made sure his handgun was locked and loaded, slipping the black Hogue .45 into his gun holder suspenders.

The Hogue .45 was Rocky's favorite gun, which he had received as a gift from Duke, for his previous birthday. Boulder put his sports coat on, hiding his guns in his gun belt and winked at his younger brother. Rocky knew this meant it was time to get his head in the game. The brothers were the first line of offense, and if their target somehow escaped from them, they knew Jacobi would get the job done, as he was the second line of offense being in the church tower.

Worm used his earpiece to confirm he had finally deciphered which room was Dr. Haven's, and congratulated himself for a job well done. He also began to cry again over his breakup with his girlfriend and Ace had to yell at him to get off the earpiece. Once, the crew had Dr. Haven's room number, they made sure to put silencers onto their guns, and looked both ways in the hallway, to ensure no maids, or guests, were around as witnesses.

Bows was ready for her part in the plan now, as she was the diversion for their mission. Her specific job was to cause a scene in the lobby, making sure if any of the guests called the front desk about strange sounds coming from Dr. Haven's room, the employees would be too distracted to deal with it.

Bows had many talents and she took pride in each of them. She could sing, dance, and act with the best of them. And it was time for a bit of acting. She had to fake a seizure and have dramatic convulsions on the lobby floor starting sharp at 10:40 a.m. She had five minutes to prepare, as she rode the elevator down to the first floor. She knew she had to be convincing, but not overly worrisome for the hotel workers because she didn't want an ambulance called over her "performance."

While Bows was walking through the lobby, wondering where the best spot for her dramatic scene should take place, Boulder and Rocky were outside Dr. Haven's suite. They had two options at this point: break into Dr.

Haven's suite with the device Worm had developed that could unlock any room in this hotel; or knock on the door and wait for Dr. Haven, or one of her companions, to open the door and invite them in.

Of course, Boulder wanted to knock first, but Rocky was afraid they'd lose the element of surprise. Boulder won out by beating Rocky in a quick game of 'Rock-Paper-Scissors.' They had 20 seconds before Bows started the distraction phase of the plan, and this would be precisely when Boulder would knock on the door.

Bows put one high heel in front of the other and walked directly up to the front desk, deciding she would get the most distraction being close to the employees, and looked at the grandfather clock placed against the eastern wall. It was time. She wasn't nervous in the slightest, for she felt at ease "on stage." She was a natural born entertainer and she craved the spotlight.

"May I help you, Mrs. Barrette?" the hotel desk clerk asked, remembering her fake name.

Bows blinked a few times, but didn't say a word before collapsing to the floor after a loud sigh. All at once, the employees came around from the desk and surrounded Bows' convulsing body. Hotel guests in the lobby shrieked at the sight of Bows on the floor. A crowd soon formed around Bows, and while she was lightly shaking and gasping for air, she was hoping Boulder and Rocky were getting the job done swiftly.

But, no one was there to open Dr. Haven's door after Boulder knocked, as Angela was in the ocean, and her bodyguards were on the beach...still searching for her.

CHAPTER 5

RUN

I. Bulls eye

"The hell with this! We don't have time to waste, let's use this gadget thingy," Rocky said, reaching into his pocket and grabbing the small device Worm had designed. It wasn't anything special; the device looked like a metal cigarette container with four neon green lights on the top. There was a faint whirring sound as Rocky placed it upon the door lock. Each neon green light shined individually for about four seconds and then the door unlocked, with a clicking noise.

Boulder grabbed the door handle and opened it slowly. The two brothers walked into the room, each holding one of their guns out in front of their bodies, ready to shoot Dr. Haven and her guests on the spot. Rocky went left, while Boulder headed towards the right, and searched the entire suite, but found no one. As soon as their search was complete, Boulder communicated to Ace that the suite was clear.

Ace ordered Boulder to stay in the room and wait for Dr. Haven to get back in case she was still making her way back into the hotel from the fire drill. He also ordered Rocky to get Bows and make their way back outside the hotel, making a perimeter spiraling away from the hotel. One way or another, Ace was going to corner Dr. Haven, and complete his mission.

Rocky made his way down to the lobby area, and spotted Bows sitting down with an icepack on the back of her neck. The hotel employees were gathered around her, making sure she was sipping the glass of water they had gotten for her. Bows spotted Rocky as he came to her aid.

"Baby, are you all right?" Rocky asked with loving concern.

"I don't know what happened, my love. I felt dizzy and collapsed, but I'm feeling much better now. Can we get some fresh air?" Bows asked.

Rocky answered, "Let's get out of here."

Rocky took Bows' hand and they walked out of the hotel and into the intense heat. They kept their eyes open, in case they were to pass Dr. Haven as they made a perimeter walk around the hotel grounds. Bows smiled to herself, knowing she had given an award-winning performance back inside the hotel and considered asking Worm to get footage from the hotel cameras so she could examine her work.

From high above their heads, Ace was watching the two lovebirds walk outside the hotel entrance and around the side of the hotel through the scope of his gun.

It would be so easy to just take that asswipe out right now...

But of course, he wouldn't do that. Still, it was entertaining to think about while he continually tried to find Dr. Haven in his gun sight.

She has to be out there somewhere.

While Ace was patiently waiting for any sign of Dr. Haven, Boulder was laying down on the comfortable sofa in the hotel suite. He decided to flip the television on and kick back for a few minutes while he waited for Dr. Haven to come back. He didn't see the harm in enjoying the air-conditioned suite while he waited for her to return.

Back in the ocean, Angela was fully relaxed. She was in cheerful spirits knowing this was exactly what she needed and didn't regret her escape for a millisecond. That was, until she squinted towards the shoreline and saw her two bodyguards standing beside her beach bag with their arms folded in front of their chests. She couldn't see their faces from as far away as she was, but she knew they weren't smiling. Funny enough, she felt like a little child who was about to get in trouble from her parents for being a bad girl.

Well, it was fun while it lasted...

Taking her sweet time, Angela swam back to the shore enjoying her freedom. She felt so miniscule in the vastness that was the ocean. Like a singular grain of sand on the beach, she felt almost insignificant. If only she could hold onto this feeling.

She swam back to the first sand bar and stood up, revealing her pale body—for she hardly had a tan being indoors most days. Angela waved to her bodyguards, who she could now see, were not smiling in the slightest. They looked pissed off, rightfully so.

Unknowingly for Angela, this was the exact moment Ace had his gun sight scanning the shoreline and Angela's waving just happened to catch his eagle-eyed gaze. Centered directly in his gun sight, Angela was waving, as if she was blatantly signaling Ace to shoot her down.

Angela continued to walk steadily back to the shore, and then began to run, splashing as much water around her torso as she could. As Ace held his steady finger on the trigger of his sniper rifle, his eyes squinted and blinked, as everything in his line of sight suddenly went dark.

There she was in all her glory. Dr. Angela Haven, a.k.a his target, centered in his sight and ready to be taken out. But in this one whimsical instant, Ace's perspective had been altered significantly. Everything, including the ocean and the people on the beach, was now a dark gray washed-out tone, and the only colorful light that was remotely visible was the gleaming illumination shining from Dr. Haven's essence. Much like Dorothy and Robert, Ace understood there was nothing more destined in this universe than his overwhelming love for this person.

It was as if Ace was in a hypnotic state watching the woman of his dreams walk to the sandy shore and out of the water. He could see the droplets of water cascading down her smooth skin and was completely mesmerized by her gorgeous glowing face. He had always seen this woman on television and in magazine covers prior to taking Pure, but seeing her magnified in his gun scope—now after he had taken Pure for himself—was a new experience he couldn't even fathom.

His target, the woman he had been hired to assassinate, was the love of his life. He knew this to be true with every fiber of his being. His finger gently released the trigger as he started to hyperventilate. He couldn't catch his breath because he knew what he had to do next. It wouldn't be an easy task, but he had had no choice in the matter. He had to act fast. Ace began to concentrate on his breathing and heard Bows' voice coming from his earpiece.

"We've spotted her, Ace. We're ready to take her out if *you* don't have a shot."

II. Make Your Move

"What in the devil were you thinking, Dr. Haven?" Mr. Hicks shouted, grabbing Angela's arm with a firm grip as she stepped onto the sandy shore.

Jacobi stepped beside Mr. Hicks, and pulled Mr. Hicks' hand off of Angela's arm straightaway. With just a scowl of his brow, Jacobi made sure Mr. Hicks knew this was an inappropriate move on his part. Like he had told Mr. Hicks before, they weren't transporting a prisoner; they were Angela's bodyguards and they shouldn't grab her in any state, unless it was out of harm's way.

As Jacobi and Mr. Hicks settled down, Angela sulked over to her beach bag and wrapped her beach towel around her slim body to dry off.

"I'm sorry, but you two didn't give much of a choice. I needed this." Angela calmly said, continuing to dry her body and soaking wet hair. She was at total ease, even though the two men in front of her were throwing shade at her.

They were all bickering over the situation at hand, not noticing Bows and Rocky were now just a stone's throw away from the trio.

"Ace, do you copy? We can take her out if you don't have the shot," Bows was informing Ace. "She's with her two bodyguards and at least one of them is packing. Rocky spotted one of them with a gun hidden tucked into his belt."

Ace hadn't stopped watching Angela through his gun sight, unable to take his eyes off this beautiful woman he felt so deeply connected to now. With his hands trembling and his focus completely askew, Ace had to communicate to his team in a composed manner.

"Everyone, listen up. Do *not* do a thing. I have this under control."

But the truth was, Ace didn't have any control over this predicament. He couldn't possibly shoot down the love of his life, and he couldn't let his crew inflict any harm upon her either. He knew if he told his crew what was really happening, they'd assassinate her anyways, because they had a mission to complete; regardless of Ace's newfound feelings.

The sweat was pouring down his face now, thinking of every possible outcome of how this could all go down. He didn't like any of the potential aftermaths.

What am I going to do? I can't watch her die. I'll kill them all before that happens.

And then it happened.

"Screw this," Rocky said to Bows under his breath. "If Ace had the shot, he'd take it. He's hesitating and I'm not going to miss our one opportunity to get it done. I want you to run back to the church, Bows."

"You heard what Ace said, Rocky! He has it under control! There must be a reason he's taking his time. Don't be a fuckup!" Bows argued.

"He's a perfectionist, Bows. He wants the credit for the textbook shot and I don't give a damn. He's wasting our time on a perfectly good day, so

I'm getting this done. Now, go!" Rocky demanded with a stern tone, pointing Bows back to the church.

Bows took a step back from her lover, watching him spin the silencer onto his gun as tight as it could go. He looked all around him, making sure there weren't too many witnesses around to see what he was about to do. Bows turned around and began to stomp away in the sand.

Rocky was a rebel and didn't care if he was going to break a direct order from Ace. Bows knew this to be true all too well and realized this would cause major drama if Rocky went against Ace's orders, so she made a judgment call of her own.

"Ace, if you don't take the shot now, Rocky is going to step up and take it. You have about ten seconds to make your move." Bows pleaded.

Of course, Rocky heard Bows on his earpiece as well, and watched as she turned her back to him literally and figuratively through this minor betrayal. But, he wasn't phased by her warning Ace; he was going through with this if the mission leader couldn't handle it. Rocky put one foot in front of the other and made his way to the trio. He only had one thing on his mind: assassinating Dr. Haven and taking out her bodyguards all in one fell swoop. No one was going to stop him.

"Rocky! I'll shoot you dead in your tracks if you take another step forward!" Ace shouted.

"Are you *really* threatening me?"

"You're damn right, I am. I'm not playing around here."

"You sure about that? By not wanting to take out our target, I couldn't be sure what type of game you're playing. What the shit is going on?" Rocky asked, now needing answers.

After hearing all of this commotion, Boulder opened his lazy eyelids from the hotel suite couch and turned the volume up a few notches on his earpiece. He was half-asleep a minute ago, but now he was wide awake and running out of Dr. Haven's room. He needed to make it to the beach quickly so he could stop his idiot brother from making a bad decision and getting shot by one of their own crew members.

Rocky stopped moving towards Dr. Haven, and turned to face the church tower. Ace had Rocky directly in his line of sight now. He was going to shoot him (or at least shoot damn near close to him) if he continued on his path towards Angela and her two bodyguards. Rocky was mad as hell now.

"Why haven't you shot her yet, Ace? Admit it; you're freezing up! I'm getting this operation done unless you take the shot—right now!"

"I'm the mission leader and it's my call. I'm not giving you the go ahead. We are aborting this mission," Ace kept Rocky in his line of sight as he communicated to everyone. "Does everyone copy?"

"What the hell are you talking about? Why would we abort the mission? This is our opportunity to take her out!" Rocky was shouting now, without realizing Angela and her bodyguards were now watching him talk to himself in a loud voice.

Jacobi was the first one of the trio to see this oafish strange looking man holding onto a gun, and instinctively knew Angela was in immediate danger. He grabbed her by the shoulders and shouted one word, "Run!"

Understandably, Angela was confused beyond words, but she knew Jacobi wouldn't shout this in her face without meaning it, so she started to run down the shore line with her beach bag over one shoulder and her towel over the other. But she didn't make it very far before she heard a single gun shot. It wasn't loud—due to the silencer—but the sound still sent a chill down her spine.

She spun around and witnessed the strange stocky man holding out his arm pointing the gun at Mr. Hicks. In an instant, Mr. Hicks collapsed on the sand, laying flat on his back. Angela's eyes squinted in the bright sunlight, and she spotted a circular formation of blood beginning to soak through his white crisp dress shirt near his heart.

And then, there were two more shots fired. This time, much louder, causing Angela to jump in a startled fashion. The shots fired were from Jacobi's gun. The first shot whizzed close by Rocky's body, while the next bullet hit Rocky square in the upper chest, causing him to tumble backwards into the sand, squirming around in agonizing pain.

With all the impulsive commotion happening at once, Ace was keeping a watchful eye on Angela, along with watching Rocky painfully rolling over on the sand. He then watched Jacobi run towards Rocky's body, and knew Jacobi would shoot Rocky dead (if he wasn't already), so Ace finally pulled the trigger on his sniper rifle, hoping he had his downrange distance correct, as well as the right amount of clicks on his scope due to the light breeze coming from the ocean.

Ace was a sharpshooter and rarely missed his target, unless he intended to, as was the case in this setting. He fired a shot just a few feet from Jacobi's feet, taking him by surprise, stopping him from pointing his gun at Rocky's head. Jacobi searched for the shooter who had barely missed his foot, but he couldn't see any other hit men on the beach aiming for him.

Jacobi wanted to finish the job with Rocky, but he got the message loud and clear from the unidentified shooter, and quickly tucked his handgun into the back of his pants. He searched the beach and realized the woman—with two bows in her hair—was watching all of this upheaval happen with her hands over her mouth. She looked terribly distraught. Bows and Jacobi made eye contact at once, and then they both ran with furious speed towards the two bodies on the sand. While Jacobi ran to Mr. Hicks, Bows ran to Rocky, each hoping the other wasn't too badly incapacitated.

Angela couldn't comprehend any of this, standing still like a frozen statue in the confusion of this horrendous moment. She didn't know whom these people were that had shot Mr. Hicks, but she didn't have time to reflect about it at this moment. All she was concerned with was keeping Mr. Hicks alive.

A shot fired directly in his heart from Rocky's gun had killed Mr. Hicks almost instantly; he was a casualty of war, and Jacobi didn't have time to grieve for his partner. He stood up and watched Angela's eyes react to the understanding Mr. Hicks was now gone. And once again, he shouted the word, "Run!"

III. Behind You

"Grab my hand!" Jacobi shouted into Angela's face while she tried to keep up with her freakishly fast bodyguard.

Running barefoot through the soft white-hot sand, Angela kept tripping herself up with her beach bag slung over one shoulder and her towel draped over the other. She considered dropping her bag and towel on the sand, but her purse and cell phone were inside her bag and she didn't want to be without these essentials.

Jacobi held Angela by the hand and was all but dragging her, being a couple strides ahead of her. He only looked back every so often to make sure they weren't being followed by the gunmen who were, without a doubt, after Angela.

"Jacobi, stop running so fast! We have to go back and try to resuscitate Mr. Hicks!" Angela was breathing hard and freaking out, barely able to yell at Jacobi, who wouldn't slow down.

"He's dead. We have to keep running until we're at a secure location. Keep up with me! We can't slow down!" Jacobi responded with not one hint of panic in his voice. He only shouted this because the beach was now in a frenzied panic from the commotion they had just left behind. The screams from the pedestrians were echoing off the waves and as Jacobi looked back, he saw a group of people surrounding Mr. Hicks' body—but he wondered why there wasn't another group of people surrounding the stocky gunman's body...

Shit. I should've aimed for that prick's head instead of his upper chest. It might only be a bad flesh wound for him.

It only took a split second before Jacobi came to the conclusion that the woman with bows in her hair must've helped the gunman get to his feet, walking him away from the scene of the crime. They could be anywhere right now. They could be with more gunmen, ready to blow Angela's head off at any given opportunity.

There was at least one more shooter...the one who shot at my feet...

As Jacobi quickly relived the experience in his head, he thought about the gunshot that nearly took his foot off. He couldn't place the shooter at the time, but since no one else was at close range to him—except for the woman with bows in her hair—he concluded it must've been a far-range shooter.

Probably a sniper from the hotel rooftop...

"Jacobi! Are you listening to me?" Angela shouted with intense fury. Her face was scrunched up grimacing in pain as she tried to pull away from Jacobi's death grip.

"What is it, Angela?"

"My foot...I stepped on a goddamn jellyfish! It stings so badly! We have to stop!"

"We can't. We have to keep going." Jacobi replied, still, with no emotion in his voice whatsoever. It wasn't as though he didn't empathize for Angela's badly stung foot, but he had a job to do. He had to protect her, no matter the circumstances.

Angela ripped her hand away from Jacobi's and collapsed on the sand. They were a few yards away from the boardwalk—which would lead them off the beach and onto the bike path, but Angela couldn't take the pain any longer.

"I can't run anymore! Mr. Hicks is dead! You're suddenly a robot man and I'm not moving from this spot until you pee on my foot!" Angela's tone couldn't be more serious, trying to catch her breath from running such a distance on the sandy shore of the beach that was, just moments ago, so peaceful.

Jacobi considered himself to be a somewhat simple individual, but he did know various things about life; such as urine *did not* help a jellyfish sting. It was a rumor perpetuated by a "Friends" episode. While Angela was trying to convince Jacobi to urinate on her foot for much needed relief, Jacobi explained to her that time, and time alone, would be the only cure for the piercing pain on her foot.

There was a small lifeguard tower just a little ways from where they were quarrelling on the beach. Jacobi noticed a bathroom facility attached to this lifeguard tower and took Angela's hand once again, lifting her up on the sand and into his arms. He carried her to this secluded spot. Once they were inside the family bathroom, Angela hobbled over to the sink. The stinging pain began to slightly subside as the adrenaline of being chased by ruthless assassins distracted her from the marginal pain she was still feeling.

Jacobi took his cell phone out and dialed the boss of his agency while Angela put her foot under the faucet, running cold water on the center of her sting. Although, the water was pouring loudly from the faucet, Angela could hear Jacobi express the upsetting news of Mr. Hicks' death to his superior. She wanted to cry just thinking about it, but she looked at her reflection in the mirror and decided she should find the courage she needed to get through this awful scenario.

Mr. Hicks gave his life protecting her, and she wasn't going to lose control now. She had to start acting as brave as possible, for the sake of staying alive. She also knew it would make Jacobi's job easier if she wasn't a frantic mess.

She washed her face after cleaning her throbbing foot, and looked at Jacobi through the mirror's reflection. He had just wiped his eyes with his hand and placed his cell phone back in his pocket.

"Are you well enough to walk on it?" he asked.

"Yes. It feels somewhat better. Where are we headed?" Angela asked back.

"As far away from here as possible. There's a boating dock down the bike path and my boss is calling in a reservation for us to rent a speedboat right now. We have to move right away."

"Then let's go." Angela responded without hesitation.

She thought this was a good plan. They'd be on the water away from any crazy people with guns. That's where she felt safest anyways—in, or on, the water. Jacobi lifted her beach bag off the floor and put it over his shoulder holding out his hand once again for Angela to take.

"Wait...put your phone in here." Angela grabbed her beach bag off his shoulder and took out a plastic pouch to store items. "We'll keep our phones in here just in case."

Angela was the type of person who was prepared for beach activities and had messed up plenty of phones due to water damage in the past until she bought this useful pouch. Jacobi was a bit apprehensive to put his phone in the pouch but knew it was perhaps a good idea. They would possibly have to get in the water at some point and it would be best to keep their phones protected.

They quickly exited the bathroom and were back on the beach. Angela buried her foot in the sand for a few seconds before jogging alongside Jacobi, hobbling on her aching foot. It felt better, but it still hurt every time she stepped on it. She concentrated on the summer heat blanketing around her body. There was a tiny relief when she felt a light breeze hitting her sweaty forehead.

Looking over at Jacobi's face, she noticed he was also sweating profusely. After all, he was wearing a suit, minus the jacket and shoes. The intense look in his eyes worried Angela. He was staring straight ahead at the boating dock sign and she knew he was thinking the same thought she was—if they could get on a boat and away from this beach, they'd be safe from the criminals that had shot Mr. Hicks.

If only…

Rocky was still in critical condition. He was in the backseat of a blacked out van being bandaged up by a freaked out Bows. They had limited medical supplies in the van but she was doing her best to stop the bleeding and bandage the wound. Driving the van was a pissed off Boulder, trying to get a hold of Ace, or Worm, on the communication devices.

But there was no answer, because at that same moment, Ace was standing behind Worm, pointing his sniper rifle directly at his head, making sure Worm wasn't going anywhere. Ace knew he needed Worm's expertise for his new task: saving Dr. Haven from his crew of highly trained assassins. Worm was confused at the events that were taking place but he also knew, even if he was armed, he wouldn't stand a chance against Ace's skillful gunmanship.

Coming to this conclusion promptly, Worm surrendered, deciding to help his mission leader, even though he knew something was completely amiss. But this wasn't the time to be asking questions and deciphering this new development—it was time to follow Ace's orders and find the location of the van through his high-tech GPS program. If Ace could locate the van and his fellow crewmembers, he'd also know where Dr. Haven was.

"What's taking so long, Worm?"

"It's tracking…they're on the move. It—it looks like they are driving down a bike path by the boating dock just a mile down from the hotel."

Ace was already packing up the equipment, ready to depart as soon as Worm had packed up his last laptop. Worm was taking his time, as he was covertly restricting Ace's communication device so he wouldn't be on the same channel as the rest of the team. He did this because he recognized Ace wasn't privy to know what the rest of the team was up to, now that he was going rogue.

Before they walked out of the church doors, Ace gave Worm a single warning, saying, "If you try to run or do anything stupid, I will kill you."

Worm nodded in agreement, grasping Ace wasn't bluffing. They bolted out of the church and found an abandoned car parked on the street. Ace chose this car to break into because it was parked there the entire morning, so he knew the driver wouldn't be coming around for it anytime soon. Between the two of them, they broke into the car and managed to hotwire it. Ace drove off like a madman on a mission—which fit his current situation completely—hoping he could make it to the boating dock before his crew did anything harmful to the love of his life.

If only…

The black unmarked van came to a screeching halt, right in front of the boating dock gates. The bikers and runners on the bike path maneuvered around the van, as Bows wiped off beads of sweat from Rocky's face, holding onto his hand, knowing he was in a sizeable amount of pain from his gunshot wound. Bows kept pressure on his chest so he wouldn't bleed out, but he was in definite need of some medical care. His pale face was not a good sign to Bows. They would need to take him back in *Sway* so Duke could help him somehow.

Bows was startled by the back doors opening, seeing Boulder move faster than she'd even known him to be because he was such a bulbous man. Wasting no time, he pulled a large metal case into his arms and dialed a five-digit code on the keypad.

The metal case opened with two high-pitched beeps and as Bows quietly whispered soothing words of comfort and encouragement into Rocky's ear, she witnessed Boulder lock and load—what looked to be—a rocket launcher. Securely resting on his large shoulder muscles, Boulder walked steadily down the boating dock ready for vengeance.

CHAPTER 6

5 STAGES OF GRIEF

I. Denial

The old man that owned the boat rental shop was leading Jacobi and Angela to their reserved speedboat at a mind-numbingly slow pace. Angela could tell by the look on Jacobi's face that he was two seconds away from pushing the old man off the dock and into the ocean, but the old man was the only one who knew which boat the keys belonged to. Angela couldn't help looking behind her, as she heard seagulls cawing and swirling around the boating office. She felt uneasy knowing there were murderers after her and Jacobi. Angela also put the pieces together in her head and figured out Mr. Hicks was an innocent casualty in all of this.

The guilt Angela felt hit her deep, but she couldn't let herself get upset about that right now. She had to focus on getting away from this beach and to a safe place with Jacobi. She looked ahead of her and watched the old man finally point to the boat Jacobi's boss had reserved just moments prior to this painstakingly dawdling march.

"I hope it's to your liking, kiddos. Enjoy some hanky panky time." The old man said with a wink. It was a bit creepy, but at the same time, it was a bit humorous coming from a man in his late 80's.

"Oh, we aren't together," Angela interjected. "Not like that."

The old man just smiled and nodded giving Angela another wink.

"Don't deny it, sweet cheeks. I can always spot love birds a mile away."

Angela contemplated on what the old man had said as he began walking down the dock at a snail's pace. She was staring at the only two visible clouds in the bright blue sky. She thought the cottony clouds resembled what could be a penguin and a cramped version of an igloo. She also thought of her former lover, Jeremy, who had taught her the childish cloud game.

I bet Jeremy would see a spaceship and a baseball cap. Or
boobs. He was always so crude playing the cloud game.

"Angela! Get in!" Jacobi bellowed, snapping Angela out of her daydreaming and back into the here and now.

Jacobi had already stepped onto the speedboat—which had the name "CHA-CHA" stenciled onto the hub. Hobbling over to the boat trying to ignore the slight stinging sensation in her foot, Angela grabbed onto Jacobi's hand and put one foot on the seat cushion, as the next foot followed. She glanced over to the old man who was not even halfway down the dock yet. The glare of the sun bounced off his shiny bald head and Angela couldn't help but notice the deep sweat stain down the back of his Hawaiian shirt from the sweltering heat.

As she stepped down from the seat cushion to the boat's base with both feet, Angela noticed another man at the opposite end of the dock. This overly muscled large man was walking onto the dock carrying something metallic-looking over his shoulder. Angela couldn't see exactly what it was from this distance, but as she waited for Jacobi to start the boat's ignition, she felt that same distressed feeling that had swirled in the air almost all day.

"Jacobi, what's that man holding over his shoulder?" she asked, pointing at the large metallic object over his shoulder.

Jacobi beheld the man Angela was now pointing at. Without any hesitation, he pulled away from the dock, ordering Angela to sit down in her seat. Almost immediately, Jacobi had recognized that the man on the dock was another hit man, and the metallic-object he was carrying over his shoulder was a rocket launcher.

Without showing any sign of panicking, Jacobi sped off as fast as the speedboat could glide through the waves, trying his best to put as much distance between the boat and the hit man on the dock. Angela hadn't known Jacobi for long; but she already recognized the solemn expression on his face covering up for something else…the look of dread.

A million thoughts ran through Jacobi's mind in a matter of ten seconds. He wondered if he'd feel any pain being blown up. He also questioned how the hit men could afford such expensive weapons. He regretted never buying a ticket to Spain, for he had longed to travel there his entire life. He thought of his time as a police officer and then transitioning to working as a bodyguard and how it all seemed so natural for him to serve and protect. He also considered Angela. And how he had let her down. They were both going to die a fiery death from a rocket explosion and he never got the chance to tell her what an amazing woman she was and how inspiring she was to him.

Sure, he knew he was evaluating their situation in a pessimistic way, but he was a realist. It was apparent they wouldn't be able to get far away from the dock when the rocket would strike the boat, hitting the gas tank and causing massive destruction—unless the hit man was a terrible shot. That was Jacobi's only hope at this point.

Please miss us…please miss us…please miss us…

Nothing in all his years of training as a bodyguard was going to help them at this point. He could swerve the boat hoping to bypass the rocket, but chances are the rocket launcher had a target-tracking device that would hit the mark no matter how hastily the boat swerved out of the way.

Boulder passed by the old man as he walked further onto the dock and didn't falter when he decided to push the old man off the dock and into the water. Stunned at the sight of the old man getting pushed into the water, Angela viewed the large man with the rocket launcher over his shoulder kneeling down on the dock, with his eye looking through the scope, locking the target-tracking sensor directly onto their boat. She knew why Jacobi was fearful now.

Oddly enough, Angela didn't have the same response as Jacobi. There was a dazed look in her eyes for a split second, and then she felt something come over her—a feeling of willpower. She wasn't fearful; in fact, she felt quite brave. She felt empowered; after all, she was on the water again, and this is where she felt the safest.

Angela grabbed Jacobi's right arm, as the wind blew her hair all around her sun-kissed face. They were speedily traveling across the ocean's wavy current, as time seemed to stretch and become boundless. Jacobi gazed into Angela's mint-green eyes and she looked right back into his, and at the same time, they both simultaneously hollered, "We have to jump!"

Angela peered over her shoulder hearing a distinct squealing noise coming from the rocket launcher. Jacobi did his best to veer the boat in the opposite direction from where they were standing ready to jump. They didn't have time to prepare, as it was a split-second decision, but they each propelled themselves off the boat's edge and jumped as far from the boat as their legs could push them. Still holding hands, they dove head first into the rough ocean water and continued to swim beneath the surface. Just a few strokes down, they felt the propulsion of the rocket's explosion hitting the boat's gas tank.

The "CHA-CHA" exploded with a powerful force, with the exception of a small fragment that was engulfed in a massive fire. The rest of the boat's remaining pieces flew in every direction in an upheaval of dispersed scorching shards.

Unluckily for Jacobi, a piece of the boat's tail-end zipped through the surface of the water and knocked him square on the back of his head, causing a gash on the right side of the back of his skull. Angela knew something was suddenly wrong, feeling Jacobi's grip loosen from her own. She opened her eyes and was shocked by the amount of blood spilling from his head at an alarming rate. She could see he was unconscious, and watched as the salty ocean water began to fill his open mouth.

Angela was hit by pieces of the boat as well, resulting in a large scrapes on her lower back and upper right shoulder—which snaked down along her right arm—but she barely felt anything more than a sizzling stinging sensation. She couldn't tell if it was the sun or the massive fire from above the surface that was lighting up the water so brightly, but she knew she had to drag Jacobi to the surface at once, without being seen by the hit man.

She knew he could just as easily shoot another rocket in their direction if he saw them come up to the surface, so she had to be as undetectable as possible. Swimming with Jacobi in her left arm, Angela quickly tried to move behind the remaining section of the boat that was still intact, but engulfed with a burning mountain of fire.

They were under water for about 20 seconds, Jacobi's mouth was still wide open, with water filling his lungs every second he was under. Angela vowed to herself that she wouldn't let Jacobi die, because he had saved her life just a short while ago.

Pulling Jacobi's body close to her own, she swam as best she could with a badly stung foot and large scrapes on her body from the explosion. Kicking as hard as she could to reach the surface, Angela could only hope she would come up behind the section of the boat that was still above the water.

Angela denied any negative thought that came to her consciousness. She didn't want to think about the fact they were at the mercy of the hit man with a fiercely deadly weapon. But she also knew, he only had a limited amount of time to stay on the dock with a weapon so large and in plain view of this horrific explosion.

The detonation was massive, and as Angela and Jacobi's heads perched above the surface of the water, there was nothing to see but the black and gray smoke that was circling around their heads. Angela could smell the burning gas and plastic and started to choke from the amount of smoke she was inhaling. Jacobi was still unconscious, so Angela knew she had to act quickly to pump the water out of his lungs.

As hard as it was to see even five feet in front of her, Angela spotted a piece of floating charred seat cushion only an arm's length away. Oddly enough, Angela's beach bag was still in one piece resting on the floating seat cushion. The bag looked burnt, but the water had splashed on it saving it from burning up completely.

From what she could tell, they were temporarily hidden from the hit man's sight; trying her best to tread water behind the enflamed section of the sinking boat. Angela swam to the seat cushion, still holding onto Jacobi's limp body, and struggled to place his neck and head onto the cushion. She began to squeeze his chest trying to use the Heimlich maneuver to remove the water from his lungs.

Dark red blood was still streaming from his head, but she couldn't concentrate on that until he was breathing again. The black smoke began to drift upwards and away from her face. Hiding behind the sinking section of the boat, she was doing her best to breathe life into Jacobi's lungs with CPR, hoping he could spit up the rest of the water, but for as many breaths as she was breathing into his mouth, he wasn't responsive.

But Angela had already made a vow to herself. She refused to give up, even while Jacobi wasn't breathing. He was slowly drifting further from her. She tried again, breathing into his mouth holding onto his nose, but this time, she pushed on his diaphragm at the same time. Without warning, Jacobi coughed up a large amount of salty water back into Angela's mouth.

Jacobi was breathing again (more so choking), and that's all that Angela cared about. She was still holding Jacobi's head above the water, but she managed to slip off the pink overshirt she had on, and wrapped it around his head. Jacobi was now breathing without choking as much, and Angela whispered in his ear,

"Thank god you're okay. We're alive."

Jacobi slowly opened his eyes and perceived Angela's angelic face just inches away from his own. He was a bit disorientated with a splitting headache, but he was now treading water on his own. He didn't need Angela's help to stay above the water's surface anymore, and without giving it another second's thought, he reached for her waist and pulled her close to him. As the last remaining portion of the boat sank into the water, Jacobi put his lips on Angela's and kissed her with a sense of uninhibited passion.

II. Anger

Ace slammed his foot on the brake pedal and the car came to a squealing halt. He put the stolen car in Park, all the while holding onto a semi-automatic gun. Understandably, Worm couldn't take his eyes off Ace's gun the entire car ride to the boat dock. He ran his shaky hand through his red mohawk and wondered how this mission went from completely under control, to completely disastrous.

Ace noticed Worm eyeing his gun, but it didn't concern him in the least bit. He knew Worm wouldn't be a fool and try anything stupid. Besides, Worm agreed to help him on his new mission; he promised Ace he was on board to save Dr. Haven from the rest of their crew—even if he did this just to save his own skin.

Directly in front of the stolen parked car was the crew's blacked out van. Ace had to play this smart and carefully, for he knew his crew were highly trained professionals, and wouldn't hesitate putting a few bullets in his chest for causing so much chaos on the beach. He didn't want to cause any more mischief, so he thought about how he'd try to convince them to lay down their weapons and stop pursuing the love of his life. Surely, Bows would understand where he was coming from. She and Rocky had fallen in love by taking Pure themselves.

I had to accept their newly found love…now they will do the same for me.

"Don't take another step, asshole!"

CLICK.

From the backdoor window of their blacked out van, Bows was now pointing Rocky's handgun at Ace's head. She was covered in Rocky's blood and had a crazed look in her golden brown eyes. She meant business and Ace knew it. He put his hands up, gun still in his right hand, and spoke as calmly as he could to her.

"Bows, listen to me…"

"I'm not listening to shit. Rocky's been shot because of you!"

"I'm sorry that happened, but—"

"But nothing! You caused this whole mission to go down in flames and you're not dragging us to Hell with you! Put your gun down and wait for Boulder to get back here. He's going to kick your ass for what happened to his brother."

"You don't understand what's going on. Let me explain!"

"Put your gun down, NOW!"

Ace didn't have a choice but to obey Bows' order. He placed the gun down by his feet and continued to raise his hands above his head.

Bows continued to say, "You can explain everything to Duke…if he doesn't kill you on the spot."

Bows shook her head in disapproval, all the while pointing the gun at Ace's head. She was mad with rage, so she wasn't thinking as clearly as she should've been. She was ready to shoot her ex-lover square in the head and she wouldn't have felt an ounce of guilt. But Ace was on an entirely different level of emotional wreckage. He wasn't enraged; he was alert and playing this as coolly as possible—for the time being.

"I want you to understand why I did this, Bows. Please listen!" Ace shouted, still holding his hands above his head. Worm was watching this happen from beside the parked car. He wanted to run away and be anywhere but the very spot he was standing. If this went down the way he envisioned, he'd be caught directly in the middle of countless bullets flying nearby.

Ace spoke up, one last time to try to get through to Bows and said, "When you and I took Pure out of curiosity, we didn't feel true love between us. You felt it with Rocky, as messed up as that was. It killed me at the time and I didn't understand it, but I get it...*now*."

Bows squinted her eyes trying to detect Ace's facial expression as he spoke these words. She couldn't figure out why he was bringing this up to her at this moment of all moments. And then it hit her like crushing weight; Ace was *purely* in love with Dr. Haven—their target.

"No...it can't be," Bows whispered.

Ace put his hands back down to his sides continuing to look into Bows' eyes from across the stretch of pavement between them.

"I have to stop Boulder from killing her, Bows. Please, put the gun down."

"You're too late," she said, pointing towards the dock.

Ace glanced over to the direction she was pointing at but couldn't see anything, due to the high fence blocking his view. He walked over to the open dock gate and saw, with his own eyes, the last of the fiery flames and the black trail of smoke coming from the destroyed boat.

Ace dropped to his knees letting out a maddened exhale, as if he suddenly couldn't take in a single breath. This was the moment he also saw Boulder walking down the dock with a rocket launcher over his shoulder. Boulder was amused at what he had just done. He had an accomplished look in his beady eyes for a job well done.

This was the moment Ace's serene attitude took a turn for the worse transforming into an enraged fury.

III. Bargaining

Angela could feel the scrape on her shoulder and her arm stinging with a blistering pain, as she made the final strokes to the furthest dock she could swim to, with Jacobi right by her side. She reached up, and grabbing the wooden spokes, pulled herself up, with the help of Jacobi's well-built arms lifting her as best he could. Once Angela was on the dock, she reached for Jacobi's hand and helped him up as well. They both collapsed onto their backs and looked up at the blue sky above. Out of breath, soaking wet, and beaten to hell, they were in mutual shock of what had just happened moments ago.

Not only did they survive a rocket launch attack, but also shared a passionate kiss. Jacobi, with his head still throbbing in pain from his deep cut, turned his head to face Angela's. She felt his glance upon her face and turned to look into his squinting eyes. Inches apart from one another, they gasped for oxygen and out of pure adrenaline and disbelief, they started giggling. Like young children, their snickering quickly turned into bellowing laughter, as they both couldn't believe their luck.

No words were exchanged for over a minute, as they caught their breath and contained themselves. Jacobi reached for Angela's face with his hand and brushed a few wet strands of hair out of her eyelashes and tucked them behind her ear. This sweet gesture caught Angela by surprise, and she sat up with a panicked movement.

Jacobi, of course, pulled his hand back and sat up slowly, realizing the romantic moment had now passed and he had to clear his head and direct himself back into survival mode. He unwrapped the pink shirt Angela had put over his head to stop the bleeding.

"I don't think that son of a bitch saw us swim away from the wreckage, but with artillery like that, he'll be coming for us again once his team realizes we aren't dead."

Jacobi was now back in *bodyguard mode* and was thinking out loud to comfort Angela.

"What do we do now?" She traced the large scrape on her arm with her shaking fingertips.

"We continue to run. Get somewhere safe. I'll call my boss and let him know what's happening. He'll direct us where to go."

"Aren't you glad I put our phones in the waterproof pouch?"

"What? Oh, yes, you saved the day." He said with a slight smirk.

Jacobi stood up and held his hand out for Angela, but she snubbed his gesture and stood up on her own, quite proud of her courage and determination to keep the two of them alive. She grabbed her beach bag and checked to see if it was still there—the picture of her and Jeremy. It was wet, but it was still in the bag. She led the way, trying to pretend there wasn't an awkward presence between Jacobi and her, but Jacobi knew she was being avoidant. They both had many thoughts to process.

> *I've made this awkward. If I could take the kiss back, I would... Shit. If I could take this whole day back, I would. I'd never let Angela go down to that damn pool. I'll never forgive myself if something happens to her. Please, god, I'll do anything to keep her safe.*

They walked down the dock, side by side, hoping they were out of sight from the hit men who were after them. Between the two of them, they covered a truckload of thoughts through their heads from survival options, to what a first kiss means after surviving an explosive boat attack? Angela was especially confused and thought about her life with each step she took.

> *I wish I could go back in time and destroy my research on Pure. I should never have developed it into fruition...if you truly do exist God, please let us get out of this alive. If you do, I swear I'll let everyone know the truth...*

The truth was, Jacobi was the only man standing between Angela and a bullet to her head, or quite possibly, a rocket. Her life depended on his professionalism and focused mind.

Sitting on a bench beside the entrance of the dock they had swum up to, was a young married couple watching the smoke billow out from the ocean waves. The concerned couple asked questions about the explosion they had witnessed moments before, but Jacobi and Angela didn't answer them. The couple didn't push it, as the wife looked in her purse for any Band-Aids she could find for any of their numerous cuts and scrapes.

Jacobi grabbed his cell phone out of the waterproof pouch and called his boss, Mr. Hornsby. The phone call didn't last long and Jacobi looked a little bit more relieved.

Jacobi reached for Angela's hand once again and she accepted, knowing he was her safety net for the time being. He didn't say a word to her, as they walked hand-in-hand in silence, keeping their eyes peeled for anyone that looked suspicious. Neither Angela nor Jacobi were particularly religious individuals, but at the same time (unbeknownst to one another), they prayed to the heavens above…bargaining with whomever was optimistically listening.

But regardless of who was listening to their prayers, their journey wasn't going to be an easy one. In fact, at that very moment, the events that were taking place would lead to quite a disruptive path for the two of them.

IV. Depression

According to Ace, Boulder had completely destroyed any chance of happiness he could've had. He shot the love of his life with a rocket launcher. There's no coming back from that. And so, Ace moved on from his shock and quiet disbelief, skipping sadness all together, and maneuvering directly to extreme anger and hostility.

Boulder was getting closer and closer to the entrance of the docking gate, and Ace was still on his knees…waiting for his chance to exact his revenge. He had to play this out carefully because he knew his team would be prepared for anything.

And now, Bows knew his truth. He had fallen in love with Dr. Angela Haven and that's why he had called the mission off. Ace couldn't hide from this truth, and he didn't care to. He wanted every single one of his crewmembers to know why he was about to kill Boulder.

In all reality, Ace couldn't really blame Boulder for doing his job because he couldn't have known Ace had fallen in love with Dr. Haven; however, he did disobey Ace's orders to stop and desist the mission. And since Boulder was the one that pulled the trigger, he was also the "someone" who had to pay.

The old man that was pushed into the water was struggling to swim to shore. He was mumbling angry insults at Boulder as he walked beside him on the dock. Boulder continued to smile looking down upon the old man in his furious state. The old man resembled a wet dog paddling to shore at an even slower speed than his walking ability. Boulder was a few feet from the dock gates when he spotted Ace on his knees, in between the blacked out van and the stolen car.

When their eyes met, Boulder knew this was going to turn into a showdown with Ace. Boulder sneered at Ace looking him dead in the eye. The maddening look in Ace's eyes frightened Bows and she knew if she didn't stop this soon, everyone on this dock would be dead.

Ace managed to get to his feet and puff out his chest as Boulder placed the rocket launcher beside the van. It clunked down with a loud bang against the pavement.

Boulder sighed and said, "You caused this madness, man. Don't blame me for getting the job done."

Ace didn't respond vocally, he just stared his opponent down ready for a battle to the death.

Ace and Boulder were now a meter away from one another with their fists clenched. Bows still had her gun pointed at Ace, but now that she put everything together, she couldn't possibly shoot him. She had to distract her team members before one of them did something they'd regret forever.

Boulder laughed and responded, "You think I'm afraid of you? You've always been a punkass. You're lucky Rocky is going to live. It's time you learned there are consequences for your actions."

Ace's gun was still at his feet, but he didn't bother trying to kick it up to his hand, although it would have been easy for him to do so. He wanted to beat Boulder to death with his fists. In a split second, they both propelled their bodies towards one another in a fit of ruthlessness. Ace was faster than Boulder and struck his nose with a powerful blow, but not without taking a brutal jab to his lower jaw.

They each backed away and raised their arms up in defense. This was going to be an old-school fist-a-cuffs battle to the death. They circled one another slowly, reading each other's faces. Boulder went in for another strike, this time driving his fist into Ace's gut with an intense force, knocking the wind out of Ace's lungs.

Ace knew Boulder had him beat if they continued to go at it this way, due to his large size. He quickly caught his breath and swerved out of the way from another powerful swing from him. Ace crouched down and swung his leg around in a swooping sidewinder kick, knocking Boulder on his back. Of course, Boulder was caught off guard by this move but dodged out of the way as Ace tried to slam his elbow into his windpipe.

Bows put her gun down and crawled to the front seat of the van. The sun was at a perfect position in the top of the sky for her to cause some distraction. As Ace and Boulder hopped back up onto their feet, they were both ready to go in for the kill. They had sparred countless times before in the training facility beneath *Sway*, so it was difficult to maneuver a solid punch when they each knew what to expect from the other. Somehow, Ace managed to get two solid punches in before Boulder side-kicked Ace directly in the chest, knocking him down on the rough pavement.

Ace acted like he was in more pain than he actually was, writhing around on the ground. Boulder came by his side and kicked him in the stomach, waiting to land another blow to his chest with a forceful stomp of his right leg. But before he could strike down on him, Ace kicked him in the groin causing Boulder to lean over in extreme pain. Ace had him right where he wanted him.

This was his chance to strike him and not let up. Arching his back and pushing off the ground with his hands in bridge position, Ace did a kick-flip to get back onto his feet. Ace was positioning himself to assault Boulder's red face with a spin-kick, but right as he was about to spin, Bows positioned the van's driver-side mirror to catch the sun's bright rays and temporarily blind Ace.

This sneaky tactic worked, letting Boulder capitalize on this without any hesitation. He wasted no time in delivering a dominant uppercut, sending Ace flying into the air resulting in his body landing hard on the pavement once again. Ace was now knocked out cold lying on the ground like a rag doll.

Boulder took this second to gain his composure. He didn't want to stop this fight until Ace was dead, but Bows shot off her gun letting him know this fight was over for now. He sneered over at her and she just shook her head in a motherly way.

"Grab him, tie him up and put him in the van. We all now how dangerous he can be," she said. "We need to take Rocky back to *Sway* for some medical assistance, otherwise he won't make it. Then we'll take care of Ace. Inform Duke we are on our way."

Bows wasn't usually the one in charge, but Boulder and Worm knew she meant business. This was a slight moment of self-satisfaction she let herself revel in. She had stopped the fight before anyone was killed, and took charge of her team. But, just as soon as that feeling crept up on her, she felt a more formidable feeling of depression.

She couldn't shake the feeling that nothing was ever going to be the same again. Her lover had been shot and was in critical condition; her ex-boyfriend was being tied up and would most likely be killed by the end of the day, and the rest of her team was falling apart. If only she could put this day away in a box forever, with a lovely bow on top.

V. Acceptance

There it was. Right when they needed it the most. It was as if the heavens above had dropped a gift on Jacobi and Angela's laps. A motorcycle, fit for two, was parked right outside the Boardwalk ice cream shop. Clearly, they would have to steal this bike, as fast as possible. Luckily for them, the key was still in the ignition. Outside the shop, people were staring at the bloody, shoeless and bruised pair as if they were extras in a zombie horror movie.

Jacobi was leading the way and nodded his head towards the bike. Angela had never been on a motorcycle in her life and felt very uneasy about this. Her feet were stinging and had started peeling from the searing pavement. The cuts on her shoulder were aching terribly. If getting on this deathtrap meant safety and medical care, then she knew she had no choice in the matter.

They both climbed on and Jacobi started the bike. The owner of this bike was walking out of the ice cream shop with two ice cream cones in his hands. He ran after the duo still clutching onto the ice cream cones and managed to throw one directly at Angela's back. Jacobi sped off onto the street with zero reluctance.

The ice cream splatter on Angela's back dripped down her spine and actually felt quite soothing on her cuts, but then began to sting with a fiery fierceness. She bit her lower lip, holding onto Jacobi's waist hoping his motorcycle driving skills were better than his boating skills. Not knowing where they were speeding towards, Angela placed her head on Jacobi's back and squeezed her eyes shut. The beach bag was still wrapped around her shoulder and swayed slightly as the bike zoomed around the cars in a speedy frenzy.

Once again, her life was in his hands and strangely enough, she felt comfortable with this fact. If anyone was going to get her through this day, it was going to be Jacobi.

The safe house Mr. Hornsby told Jacobi about was 45 minutes away. Jacobi stepped onto the accelerator zooming through the traffic. Angela held onto Jacobi tighter as she watched the beach pass her squinty eyes. She thought she was going to spend her day in the ocean; but instead, she was running from assassins holding onto her bodyguard, zigzagging through the traffic, to an unknown location.

At least we'll be safe…

Funny how things don't always go the way you think they will.

Meanwhile, Mr. Hornsby was walking down his porch stairs to his private beach along the ocean. Fifty-four years old, but looking much younger with a full head of brown curly hair and good looks, Mr. Hornsby looked like a modern day movie star. He held a glass of expensive whiskey in his hand and sipped on it, as he searched through his recent phone calls. He found the name he had called just moments ago, except no one answered.

Jacobi had called him just 20 minutes prior, and informed him one of his agents was dead. Mr. Hicks, one of Mr. Hornsby's first hires, was a loyal agent; did his job better than most. Mr. Hornsby had owned his bodyguard protection agency for over 20 years and Mr. Hicks had been his first agent to die on the job. He was a fine agent, but an even better friend and confidant. The risk of death was always a formidable consequence of this profession, but it had never become an actuality in all the years of his owning the agency.

Through all the years of owning this company, Mr. Hornsby had made a significant amount of connections. Even before he owned his own agency, he had made connections, propelling him into the position and wealth he had always desired. The first connection he had made, contributed the money to start up his own agency. This was from the man he didn't want to contact at the moment. He wasn't necessarily a friend of his, but he was a man who he owed his wealthy lifestyle to. This man's name was Duke Harrington.

Mr. Hornsby had worked for Duke Harrington back in the day and when he started his own company, Duke had lent him the start-up money to help him create a successful business. Mr. Hornsby had always been a reliable source for Duke and vice-versa. They were never particularly great friends, but they understood one another. Duke was on the wrong side of the tracks and Mr. Hornsby had made a legitimate business, but they both needed one another's assistance from time-to-time to get their "jobs" done.

This was one of those times.

When Duke heard Dr. Angela Haven had bodyguard protection around her, he immediately called Mr. Hornsby on a secure line, to see if he was hired to protect her. Normally, Mr. Hornsby wouldn't be able to divulge this information to anyone, but he never kept information from Duke. He told him his best agents were on the job. He was in a compromised position; being hired to protect a celebrated scientist, but also being a loyal associate to the man who he owed so much to.

He didn't have much of a choice at this point, he had to give Duke the details he had requested. He gave up some of the information, including the hotel they were staying at. In his guilty-conscious mind, he thought if they wanted her, they'd have to work for it in some regard, so he kept the room number to himself as well as other bits of knowledge—as if keeping these small details from Duke and his team would absolve him from being the traitor he was.

He gave up this information under one condition: his agents would never be in danger, in any way. Duke had agreed to this, not knowing how out of control his team would be once their mission was under way. It should have been no problem for his team of assassins; but that was before Ace had gone rogue.

Mr. Hornsby called Duke again, but still, there was no answer. He was starting to get quite vexed, knowing Duke was avoiding his call. Duke had promised his agents would be safe during the mission and now one of them was dead, while the other was seriously injured. He called Duke once more and when he still didn't answer, Mr. Hornsby downed his glass of whiskey and whipped the empty glass into a cluster of rocks by the steps of his home. Just then, his phone began to ring and he answered it.

"You screwed me, Duke." He said, grating his back molars together.

"I know this wasn't part of the arrangement. I am utterly apologetic by the events that have taken place and—"

"Shut the hell up! One of my best friends is dead! He didn't deserve to die because of your team's screw-up!"

"I apologize profusely. That should never have happened and there will be consequences for their actions…"

"Damn right, there will be!"

"And of course, retributions will be made to you and your agency. I would hate to see our partnership ruined by today's catastrophic events."

"What happens next, Duke? I can't even think straight right now. I betrayed my agents and our client, and if this comes back to me—"

"It won't; let's calm down. It's done. I've spoken to my team and they have everything under control again. We had a rogue member of the squad that was put down, and a rocket launcher, of all things, was used to execute our target. So, you see? Everything worked out in the—wait. Did you say only one of your bodyguards was dead?"

"Yes. And what are you talking about, Duke? Dr. Angela Haven is still alive. She's still with my other bodyguard as we speak."

Duke was quiet for a few seconds, not knowing what to say. He thought Boulder had killed them both when he had fired the rocket launcher onto the boat they were on. Duke paused and took a deep breath. He accepted the mission wasn't quite over yet and continued to speak to Mr. Hornsby, for he needed more information to continue moving forward.

"No shit? They survived that attack? I'll be damned. I guess this mission will be tougher than I had anticipated."

"Your mission is over, Duke! I'm not putting my agent in danger again."

"Listen, we are so close to completing this operation. Don't lose faith in us now. Just tell us where those two have run off to and we will end this once and for all."

"Duke, I can't be—"

"You owe me this one last favor. Just tell me where they are going and you won't hear from me again."

Mr. Hornsby gave this a moment's thought while contemplating all the intellectual pros and cons he could make in his semi-drunken state. By the end of the phone call, he caved in and gave Duke the whereabouts of the safe house. But not before getting a large sum of money transferred to the offshore account in his name.

Mr. Hornsby walked back up the porch steps and stepped on a piece of broken glass by the rocks. His foot was bleeding, but he could barely feel it as he walked inside and poured himself an even larger whiskey. He looked at his reflection in the mirror and didn't recognize the man looking back at him.

What have I done?

For a brief moment, he contemplated playing both sides and warning Jacobi that he was in danger from the same assassins that had almost killed him earlier. He wanted to reach out, especially on behalf of Mr. Hick's. But he didn't.

He poured another drink for himself and stared out into the ocean from the inside of his glass house. He had accepted he was just as bad a person as Duke was. He let everyone down. Especially himself.

CHAPTER 7

DOWN THE BEATEN PATH

I. Business is Business

Ice-cold water splashed Ace's face waking him up to the dull pain in his head. It felt like his skull was put in a vice grip and was squeezed to the max. His right eye was swollen shut and his body was aching from the hand-to-hand brawl he had just lost to his fellow team member. Out of his left eye, Ace could see Boulder sitting in front of him straddled on a wooden chair. His face was also swollen from the fight and his knuckles were still bloody, but he didn't show any signs of pain.

Using all his might, Ace tried to move his arms from behind his back, but couldn't because his hands were tied with rope, secured around his wrists. His feet were also roped to his chair and there was a long piece of duct tape wrapped around his head covering his mouth. He was not in a good position to escape, fight or maneuver out of this predicament.

Bows was standing behind Boulder tapping her foot on the dusty cement floor. There was a soft echo from the patter of her high-heeled shoes, and even though Ace was in immense pain from the fight, the sound of this constant tapping was causing him more annoyance and discomfort than his physical pain. If only he could say what he wanted to. He'd let his "team members" know exactly where they could go.

"It didn't have to come to this, Ace. I couldn't put my finger on it. Why would our team leader go through all this trouble to stop our mission? It didn't make sense. But Bows has an interesting theory..."

Oh, Jesus, listening to Boulder's condescending speech is agony. Please just shoot me in the head.

"Stop talking, Boulder. Let's just sit in silence while we wait for Duke to call us back with our instructions," Bows quipped, without looking Ace in the eye.

She purposefully looked down at her feet because she was ashamed of what she was saying. Everyone in this room knew what Duke's orders were going to be. Worm was hunched over on the floor resting his head against the concrete wall. He couldn't look Ace in the eye either.

Ace couldn't figure out what this small space was until he tried focusing his eyes—even the swollen shut one—and realized they were in a mausoleum. As mausoleums went, this one was on the larger and more expensive side. Whoever was buried here, it seemed as though they were of a lofty and lavish family that dedicated quite a bit to their final resting place. He focused his line of sight on the only stained-glass window in the concrete box. He could tell not much time had passed since he was knocked out since the sun seemed to still be shining brightly.

Mumbling, Ace tried to let his team know he had something to say. Boulder just smirked from his chair and cupped a hand to his ear trying to make out what he was saying.

"Oh for God's sake!" Bows shouted. She began to walk over to Ace, but Boulder grabbed her forearm.

"What are you doing?"

Unbeknownst to Boulder, Bows had a pocket knife in her other hand, which she slipped right under Boulder's neck.

"Get your hand off of me…now." Bows was not in the mood for this and pressed the blade of her knife with just enough force to let Boulder knew she meant business.

Boulder let go of her forearm and Bows put the knife by her side once again. She kept her beautiful brown eyes on Boulder, as she walked over to Ace. She cut the piece of tape that was wrapped around his head and threw it on the ground.

"Thank you, Bows," Ace said in a barely audible voice, as he needed a drink of water. "As I was trying to say before, this whole situation has gotten completely out of hand."

"Understatement of the year, buddy boy," Boulder said with a laugh.

"I can explain my actions and maybe then, you'll see—"

"We'll see what? How you betrayed the mission? Or how you betrayed us?" Bows asked.

She was ready for Ace to explain himself, even though she knew quite well what his explanation would be.

"Funny that you, of all people, would feel betrayed, Bows. After what you did to me."

"I didn't *do* anything to you, Ace. You know how the drug works! It's not—" Bows immediately shut her mouth. She knew he had tricked her to say exactly what he needed her to.

"It's not, what? It's not our fault that Pure changes the way we feel for certain people? Like the way you fell for Rocky," Ace paused for a second, and looked directly into her eyes. "Or the way I fell for Dr. Haven?"

Worm stood up now and was fidgeting back and forth like he was trying to solve an intense mathematical equation.

"So, it's true, then? You fell in love with our target? Pure affected you, too. But don't you see? This is why we have to kill her, Ace. Her drug causes massive problems. Look at the situation you're in now! Duke is going to kill you because of this. And we can't help you." Worm was saying this from afar, because he didn't have the fighting skills like his other team members and even if Ace was tied up, he couldn't trust being close to him.

"You are all cowards. Especially you, Bows. I thought of all people who would understand where I'm coming from, it'd be you."

Now Ace was the one that couldn't look his team in their eyes. Not because he was ashamed of himself, but because he was so ashamed of them. He always knew this group of people would never be considered humanitarians of the year, but he thought he was part of their dysfunctional family. He now knew he was wrong.

Everyone sat in silence for a moment or two before the mausoleum door creaked open. And there standing in front of the bright sunlight was their boss. Duke walked in wearing his traditional trench coat and nodded his head signaling for the team to get lost. Worm was the first to exit. Boulder followed next, but not before Duke grabbed him by the shoulder leaning in close.

Duke whispered in his ear, "Get it done this time, no matter what. I've texted you the address."

"Yes sir. How's my brother doing?"

"I called Dr. Peterson as soon as you all took him back to *Sway*. My doctor is the best there is concerning gunshots. He'll pull through."

Bows was the last to make her way towards the door, but before she walked out, she made her way back to Ace and bent close down to his face and kissed him on the cheek. They looked into each other's eyes longingly and then she walked away from him, leaving Duke and Ace alone.

"Well, my boy. I never thought it would come to this." Duke stepped around the dusty cement surface in front of Ace. He wanted to look him directly in the eyes at this moment.

"Duke, please—"

"Oh no. Don't embarrass yourself, Ace. Begging won't get you anywhere with me, as you know damn well who I am and how I handle betrayal," Duke was now a foot away from Ace, as he held his face in his hands. "You were my favorite. I'm telling you this because you need to know I don't find any pleasure in killing you. But, business is business." Duke fished around in his trench coat and found his handgun. He cocked it and held it close to his hip.

"That's bullshit, Duke. You don't have to do this. I took the drug; when Bows and I were together. We wanted to prove it to one another we were meant for each other, but as you know, it didn't work out that way. But, I found her today. The love of my life!"

"Yes, I know, the doctor, Angela Haven, also known as, our target. And, what a shame that is. Life can be so cruel." Duke said this in a condescending manner.

Without any warning, Duke struck Ace in the face with the back of his hand. He held his gun up to Ace's forehead and exhaled.

"That damn drug…I just want *you* to know, I *am* sorry for this, but I did warn you to get the job done." Duke said this with tears in his eyes. He looked genuinely sad about what he was about to do.

Little did Duke know, Ace had been cutting through the ropes on his hands the entire time Duke was chatting it up with him. Before Bows left the mausoleum, she had kissed Ace on the cheeks and secretly placed her pocketknife in his hand. Ace was shocked by this turn of events, but didn't question her motives. Maybe she pitied him or maybe she realized he was in the same boat she was when she couldn't control whom she loved once upon a time.

Either way, Ace made the most of his time with that knife, and just in the knick of time, cut through the ropes and maneuvered out of the way, as Duke shot the gun off, hitting the tomb inside the mausoleum.

Ace used all his might to stab Duke right in his left shoulder, causing them to fall back against the cement wall. With his quick reflexes, Ace twisted the knife in Duke's shoulder and wrestled the gun out of his hand. Duke wasn't the type to beg for his life, but he knew Ace had him cornered. Holding his right arm up, he silently pleaded for Ace to back away, but Ace wasn't having this. He pointed the gun up to Duke's temple and wiped the bloody pocketknife on Duke's jacket, then put it in his front pant's pocket.

Leaning his head close to Duke's face, he whispered, "I just want *you* to know, I'm *not* sorry for this…"

WHACK!

It happened so fast; Duke didn't have time to be scared. Ace spun the gun around in his hand and pistol-whipped him in the side of the head, knocking Duke unconscious.

Ace didn't waste a second dragging Duke to the chair and tied his boss up with the same rope he had just cut off from his hands. The rope was shorter now, so there was only enough length to do a quick knot, but this would give Ace some invaluable time to find his team and save Dr. Haven in the process.

Before leaving Duke, he checked his coat pocket and found his phone. He looked up the latest text message to Boulder, and now he knew the exact address of where his team was going. They had a bit of a head start, but nothing was going to stop him from going down the beaten path and righting the wrongs that were happening on this day.

He didn't want to kill any of his team members, but he would do what was necessary, if it came down to it. Ace contemplated killing Duke right then and there, but he knew his team members would hold that against him. If he was in a real bind, maybe that'd be the ticket to have in his back pocket, to convince his team members to let Dr. Haven walk away from all of this.

If only he could convince them how he felt about her. They were assassins, but they had hearts. Look at how devastated Worm was today. Maybe they weren't exactly his friends, but he could appeal to their humanity, and hopefully, they would follow some municipal assassin rules: such as, don't kill your other team member's love interests.

After all, business is business.

II. Cry Just a Little

The wind was whipping through Angela's hair as the motorcycle twisted and turned, propelling the two down the highway pavement. The sun was still shining down on Los Angeles, but the temperature was holding at a sweltering 94 degrees. Never in a million years did she think she'd be on the back of a motorcycle on this day, let alone ever. Jacobi shifted gears and drove off the next exit of the highway. He seemed to know exactly where he was off to, like he'd been to this location a few times before.

Driving down what looked to be a typical suburban road, where every house looked exactly the same, Jacobi was doing his job of looking for any suspicious activity. But to the casual eye, nothing seemed out of the ordinary. Children played in their front lawns and neighbors were cutting their grassy lawns.

Angela didn't feel so out of place here, as she was still wearing her swimsuit underneath her jean shorts and crop top. Most of the neighbors they had passed by were in their bathing suits as well. Lighting off fireworks that were leftover from July 4th on their driveways. The popping sounds made Angela jump a few times thinking it was the sound of gunshots.

Across the street from where Jacobi was slowing down, was a house that looked under construction. It looked like an old house had been bulldozed and what was left was just a junkyard of a construction site.

As the motorcycle slowed down, Angela felt quite relieved when they finally pulled up to one of the basic-looking houses on this suburban street. They had made it to the safe house. Jacobi pulled up into the driveway and parked the motorcycle, helping Angela off the bike.

They walked up to the front door, but this door was not like any of the other front doors on this block. It didn't have a key lock, but a number pad on the side. Jacobi pressed a series of numbers, pushed his hand onto the gel pad, and the door unlocked with a soft beeping chirping sound.

Walking into this house, Angela already felt a sense of safety. The windows were barred and after Jacobi shut the door, it automatically locked with steel reinforcements. This place was more than just a suburban safe house. There was no way anyone could get through the front door. Angela tried to observe the layout of this house.

The first thing Angela noticed after walking through the front door was a beautiful chandelier hanging from the ceiling in the foyer. It wasn't overkill, it was just right for this space. Standing in the foyer, Angela looked at the staircase to the second floor leading to a long hallway. The brass railing looked old and dusty, completely out of touch with the rest of the modern looking interior. The ceramic tile under Angela's bare feet felt cold and gave her a sense of soothing relief that she didn't know she was so desperately in need of. She looked down at the partially bloody footprints she was trailing behind her and apologized to Jacobi. He scoffed as if that were the least of their worries—which was completely true.

He walked Angela into the dining room, just to the left of the staircase. Angela peered out the large window looking into the front lawn. She smiled holding onto the bars that covered this window. This place was virtually a fortress and she could finally feel a sense of safety that she hadn't felt the entire day while they were on the run.

Jacobi showed her the adjoining family room that was bare in decorations, but oddly there were hundreds of cluttered newspapers on the large sofa. There was a television mounted on the wall, but nothing else was in the room. This room was attached to the kitchen, which was small in size, but very contemporary in design.

"Make yourself at home," Jacobi said, with a small smirk on his face.

He started piling the newspapers off the couch and onto the floor to make room for them.

"I think this is the first time I've seen you smile all day. It's kinda nice."

Obviously, Jacobi didn't know how to respond to this, so he used his stoic nature to fill in the silence. Clearing his throat, he grabbed the remote off the sofa and turned the television on.

"Can't wait to watch some 'Judge Judy,' huh?"

Angela took a seat on the sofa and realized just how tired her aching body was from all the torment it had experienced thus far.

"What do you have against 'Judge Judy'? I wanted to show you all of the camera feeds in this place. Outside and in, so we can both keep watch. I'm confident those people couldn't have followed us here, but just in case they do happen to find us, I'd like to be prepared." Jacobi said, pointing to the television, flipping through the channels.

Jacobi flipped back and forth from three different screens of camera feeds. Each screen was a display of the 6 different rooms of the house, or of the various angles of the front and back lawns. The entire property was on camera and no one was getting in without heavy artillery.

After Jacobi showed her the camera feeds, Angela made her way to the kitchen and looked in the fridge. It was stocked with frozen TV dinners and water bottles. She spotted some microwaveable popcorn and knew what her dinner would consist of.

"How long are we staying here for?" she asked.

"When we get word from my boss that we are no longer in danger. Then we can move on, but this is the safest place for us to be in for the time being. If you go upstairs, there should be clothes for each of us to change into. Check the closet in the master bedroom. After we both get washed up, I'll show you all the in's and out's of this place. There's even a panic room in the basement." Jacobi said.

"I'm claustrophobic." Angela stated matter-of-factly.

Jacobi just stared at her face blankly until she smiled. She dug through her beach bag and handed him his phone. There was no reason to keep their phones in the waterproof bags anymore. Angela made her way back to the foyer, walking on the sides of her feet since she didn't want to bloody up the tiled floor anymore than she already had.

Angela made her way up the staircase holding onto the banister railing. Each step up was a tiny struggle for her aching body. She peeked her head into the first room she came across in the long hallway. It was a guest bedroom with a full size bed, a dresser and a television hung on the wall. There was also a strange looking plant placed in the corner of the room, oddly out of place.

Angela placed her beach bag down in the hallway, and looked into the guest bedroom again, this time noticing something on one of the plant's stems. There was a white piece of paper attached to it and Angela's curiosity got the best of her. She walked into the room and knelt beside the plant to read the note.

You are safe here.

She smiled to herself, knowing this was true. As she began to stand upright, a slight metallic glimmer in the dirt of the plant caught her eye. She moved a bit of the dirt away with her hand and slowly pulled out a small handgun buried in it. She brushed it off, looked around the room and up at the small camera in the top corner of the bedroom. There was a red light blinking from it and she knew Jacobi was probably watching her at this very moment. She placed the gun back into the dirt and covered it up. She brushed her hands off and walked out of this room, picking up her beach bag and continued down the hall into the master bedroom.

This room was a bit more decorative, with paintings on the wall and a coffee table with a tea set resting upon it at the foot of the bed. The carpet felt nice on her swollen feet and without any hesitation, Angela collapsed on the comfortable king size bed. She rested there for a couple minutes grabbing onto one of the pillows. Everything smelled fresh and clean—unlike her own body odor.

She managed to get back on her feet and walked directly to the closet. It was much bigger than she had anticipated. Half of the closet was filled with men's clothing and the other side was filled with female clothing options. The choices were of limited size and fashion, being mostly suit jackets and pant suits but at least these options didn't have blood stains and sweat in every fiber. As opposed to the clothing she and Jacobi had been wearing most of the day.

Angela searched through the clothing options and found a black pants suit and some new undergarments that were practically her size. She grabbed all the articles of clothing and made her way to the master bathroom. She began to run the water for a bath as she undressed. She looked at her naked body in the mirror and was surprised to see all the cuts and bruises. The adrenaline had made her oblivious to most of the smaller cuts on her body from the boat explosion.

Easing her beaten up body into the warm water, she felt a stinging sensation in every inch of her skin. Not only was this bath necessary to clean the scrapes on her body, but it was needed to calm her nerves. Angela's stress levels were at breaking point and this calming bath was the first chance she had to catch her breath and process the insane events of the day.

She thought about Mr. Hicks and how he had died on the beach. She was helpless to save his life and the image of his body was permanently stuck in her mind. A few tears dropped from her eyes as she sank under the bath water.

Downstairs, Jacobi was inspecting every corner of the house, making sure all the components of the security systems were working properly. When he was satisfied, he went to the bathroom and looked into the mirror. He used his phone to help him see the back of his cut up head. The cut from the boat explosion wasn't too bad, it had stopped bleeding, but he needed to put a fresh bandage on it. He grabbed the first aid kit from the kitchen pantry and scoffed at the lack of bandages. There was one butterfly bandage perfect for his wound.

After securing the bandage on the back of his skull, he called Mr. Hornsby to follow up. Mr. Hornsby told him they'd have to spend the night there, until his private jet could be ready to take both Jacobi and Angela to another country for the time being.

Obviously, Mr. Hornsby felt extremely guilty about giving Duke the whereabouts to the safe house and wanted to warn Jacobi about it, but he knew he couldn't double cross Duke. After all, Duke had promised Jacobi would be safe when they infiltrated the house. The mission was to kill Dr. Haven. And he could live with that betrayal.

After the phone call, Jacobi flipped through the camera feed on the TV and clicked on the master bedroom. Angela was standing by the bed in her bath towel, brushing her hair. She put the hairbrush on the nightstand and dropped her towel. Jacobi looked away while she put her clothes on, as he was a gentleman.

Angela was now dressed and feeling like a new woman. She rummaged through her beach bag and grabbed her cell phone. She called her parents and told them all about the horrible events of the day, and advised them to get somewhere safe immediately. She felt much better knowing they were out of harm's way since they were practically the only family she had.

She went through her texts and realized she didn't have many close friends these days, besides her coworkers. She scrolled down and found Jeremy's name. The man "from her past." The man in the picture Jacobi had dropped at her house.

Before leaving her hotel suite, Angela made sure to bring the picture of Jeremy into her beach bag. It was an important picture to her, and she wanted it close. Looking at this picture brought up so many memories and she realized she wanted to hear his voice more than anything at this moment. So, she clicked on his name and decided to give him a call. She let it ring three times before Jeremy picked up.

Jeremy answered, "Hello?"

Angela wanted to say so much to her former lover, but no words came out.

"Angela? You there?" he asked.

Still, Angela couldn't bring herself to say a single word. She ended the phone call and began to cry, once again. The tears were coming down fast now and Angela slid off the bed, onto the carpet floor. She sat there sobbing quietly into her hands.

Still watching the camera feed, Jacobi could see Angela was holding onto the picture of the mysterious man. He wanted more than ever to ask her about him, but he knew it wasn't his place. He also knew he couldn't shower and change until she had gotten herself together.

It was only minutes later when Angela came down the stairs with a random makeup bag and told Jacobi the shower was all his.

"Do you know whose makeup bag this is? I found it in the bathroom."

"It's one of our previous client's. She left it here for the next girl that had to escape from her abusive husband. I'm going to clean up now. I'll be quick."

Jacobi placed his hands on Angela's hand as a comforting gesture.

"Oh, please, take your time. That bath was practically spiritual; it felt so good," Angela said, slipping out of his hands to begin applying eyeliner. "Oh, and I left some antiseptic lotion on the counter, for any cuts you might have to clean up."

"Appreciate it." He said, walking out of the room and up the stairs.

Angela sighed watching his large-framed body walk away. She actually loved feeling his hands on hers, but at the same time she felt uncomfortable not knowing if he had regretted kissing her by the dock explosion. Plus, her flirting skills were not topnotch these days.

Jacobi started to unbutton his shirt and plopped it down on the coffee table. He did the same face plant onto the bed as Angela had just done. He needed a minute to feel nothing but the cozy mattress and clean sheets against his body. He smelled a hint of vanilla and lavender coming from the bathroom. The scent seemingly was getting stronger as he walked into the bathroom and saw a dimly lit candle casting various shadows on the wall. Angela had lit a candle to set the mood to her bubble bath.

It's funny how comfort can transition your mind from survivor mode, to contemplation mode in a matter of seconds. Jacobi was now contemplating the kiss he and Angela had shared just a few hours ago. He wondered if she was thinking about it as much as he had been.

And Angela was thinking about their kiss in that same moment. But, she was also thinking about Jeremy now. The two of them shared a past. He had been the love of her life—thus far. They celebrated holidays, weekend trips to Napa Valley, and snuggled in bed taking turns making breakfast for one another each Sunday morning. Angela thought this man would be her husband. But sometimes, life has other plans for you.

In fact, after the demise of that relationship, she buried herself in her career and hadn't dated another man since Jeremy. Reporters and TV producers all wanted the scoop on Dr. Haven's love life—obviously because she was the creator of the one and only love drug on the market. But Dr. Haven never revealed details about her personal life, mostly because she didn't have much of one.

There were a few reporters who snooped into her life and found Jeremy to interview. He was always kind enough to Angela not to reveal anything about their relationship, no matter how much money was thrown in his direction. The two of them knew the details that led to their split, and they were the only people that needed to know what transpired.

After Angela put on some makeup and looked presentable, she threw some popcorn in the microwave and preheated the oven for a frozen pizza she would "prepare" for Jacobi. This was about the extent of Angela's cooking skills, as she never had the time to cook a proper meal being in the lab so many hours of her waking life.

Meanwhile, Jacobi found some clean clothes to put on after his relaxing shower and found an extra gun clip in the safe that was hidden in the master bedroom. He took a few deep breaths, feeling a bit queasy. He was getting hungry, having not eaten anything since breakfast.

Too bad this was the exact moment the assassins had pulled up to the next-door neighbors home. Jacobi wouldn't have a chance to eat his pizza.

He would be much too busy in a matter of minutes.

III. Games Children Play

Bows was the first to exit the blacked-out van. She was wearing an all black outfit that matched everyone else's apparel on the team. Except she made some last minute touches to make the getup more feminine and fashionable. Her hair was in a tight high ponytail accentuated with a glittery bow, and her lipstick was a shade of dark maroon that resembled a dried-blood color. She had a single hand knife wrapped around her calf, whereas Boulder was armed with several handguns and knives on his utility belt and attached to his bulletproof vest. Worm opened his metallic steel briefcase and grabbed a couple of gadgets that resembled something out of a *James Bond* novel.

Once all three of the team members were outside the van, they made sure to test their earpiece communication devices. Boulder made a series of hand signals to Bows and Worm and crept to the side of the house. Bows looked at Worm and they both shrugged their shoulders, as neither one of them knew how to interpret what his hand signals meant.

Worm led Bows to the front door and attached the first gadget on it right above where the door handle should've been. Since this front door was made to keep intruders out, Worm had quite the challenge opening this door to the fortress. But if anyone could figure out an electronic way of getting inside, it would be him.

"Here, take this. All you have to do is attach it to a door and twist it counter-clockwise. And make sure you move out of the way." He said, handing Bows a circular metallic device. Bows put it in her back pocket and stepped away from Worm, letting him do his thing.

Bows looked around the house for any drainpipe or ladder she could climb to a second story window to get inside. But as she examined the windows, she realized they were barred. There would be no getting in through a window to this safe house. Even the window wells to the basement were blocked off, filled with cement.

Bows made her way to the backyard and spotted Boulder crouching down beside a tall tree. She put her hand over her eyes to block the bright sun. The twilight hour was approaching in a few hours time and the sun was at that angle where it was in your eyes no matter where you stood.

Once Boulder made eye contact with Bows, he rolled his eyes and signaled for her to come behind the tree with him. She slowly walked towards the tree as he was mouthing the words, "Move! Get over here!"

She didn't understand the urgency and outrage he was displaying in a mime-like form. He pulled her behind the tree's large trunk and scolded her for not following his direct clear hand signals to stay low and stay hidden until Worm could get the front door open. She pushed Boulder away from her as best as her tiny frame could push a 230-pound mountain of a man. She stood behind him and lit a cigarette, intentionally blowing the smoke in his direction, knowing he couldn't stand the stench.

Off the second story master bedroom, there was a small balcony made out of some sort of wood with iron reinforcements. The door to the balcony was made of some sort of Plexiglas and from what Bows could tell, it didn't look as if there were any bars covering it. If they could find a ladder of some sort, they could get into the safe house that way.

Worm's gadget was working on decoding the door's internal locking mechanism. It was now at 14% and counting. This would definitely take some time. So, meanwhile, Worm got onto his tablet and began hacking into this particular street's electrical system.

Worm was observant enough to realize there were cameras everywhere on this safe house—inside and out. If he could shut the electrical grid down for the entire street, at least the cameras wouldn't capture his team trying to get inside. For all he knew, the doctor's bodyguard could've spotted them already. If he could just shut down the grid, the cameras would be shut down and they'd be free to roam around and get in the house without being seen.

He had just hoped they hadn't yet, for the surprise attack could be their only chance to kill this horrible woman causing all the trouble today. The more he thought about it - their situation - the more Worm felt sickened by this whole scenario. He felt a connection to his team members, for they had each saved his life on multiple occasions (especially Ace), and he was completely uncomfortable with the idea that there was a battle going on amongst them.

He was torn because he understood why the mission had to be completed, but he also felt sorry for Ace. They all understood why he didn't want to complete the mission because he was in love with the target. But Worm had a job to do and couldn't let his friendship with Ace get in the way of it—no matter how badly it hurt him to do so.

22%...damn it! Let's go! We don't have time to wait.

Angela had her back to the television screen, as she chomped down on her big bowl of freshly made microwavable popcorn. She looked for some butter to melt but there was none in the fridge. She also looked for salt in each cabinet with no luck. The TV dinner was still thawing as it had been in the freezer for probably many months now.

Angela could hear the shower running above her in the master bathroom. She was imagining scenarios of Jacobi coming downstairs in just his towel and grabbing her by the waist, pulling her close to his wet body and giving her another kiss—this time leading back up to the bedroom. She shook her head and tried to get this image out of her mind.

It's just been a while. You are not attracted to Jacobi... You are not attracted to Jacobi...Oh, just be real with yourself. He's sexy as hell. Of course you are attracted to that man! Just be cool. Play it cool.

But playing this cool was never Angela's strong suit. Even when she would get hit on in her college days by other swimmer's on the men's team, she couldn't quite find the right words to say. Some of her friends would tell her she was too 'book smart' to flirt smoothly. And, there definitely was some truth to that. She smiled to herself hoping Jacobi had any sort of inkling of the sort of feelings she was experiencing. They hadn't known each other for more than two days, but they had already been through so much together. If there was ever any future for the two of them, at least they'd have an interesting story of how they met.

Angela grabbed the bowl of popcorn off the kitchen counter and spun around on her toes facing the living room. Right as she spun, the television clicked off. She looked at the microwave clock and it was shut off as well.

That's strange.

Chewing on her popcorn, Angela noticed how quiet this safe house could be. She could hear Jacobi shutting the shower off from directly above her. She was happy Jacobi took his time finally getting to recuperate. This relaxation time was crucial for both of them. He called down to Angela and told her he'd be just a few moments longer. She told him she had already started on dinner and jokingly told him to wear his nicest suit.

Meanwhile, Worm told his team members the cameras were now shut down and Boulder felt it was safe for Bows and himself to step away from the tree. He ran around the house and back into the front lawn, watching Worm do his thing. Worm signaled Boulder to come over to the front stoop of the house.

"It's not working, man." Worm said hesitantly.

132

"What do you mean? It says 22%. That piece of shit working, or not?"

"It's been stuck there for over five minutes. I think the safe-lock door is too sophisticated for this unlocking mechanism. And that's saying a lot because this bad boy cost Duke a pretty penny."

This did not please Boulder. He was determined to get inside this house somehow. And just as Jacobi and Angela were handed a gift from the heavens with the stolen motorcycle, Boulder found a gift too good to be true. There it was, across the street in the neighbor's backyard.

The house across the street was practically demolished. There were several construction machines for the taking. The one that caught Boulder's eye was the bulldozer with the attached scoop. This particular machine was designed to 'scoop,' or shovel large amounts of the ground material and place it in a pile.

Boulder smiled slyly and said, "I'll be right back, Worm."

He was definitely up to something as he crossed the street and disappeared for a few quick minutes. Worm was still stressing out about his gadget and was ready to contact Duke to let him know they had failed to get into the safe house, when he heard a loud rumbling noise coming from across the street.

There was Boulder, driving the four-wheel scoop across the front lawn of the neighbor's property and down onto the street. He was going as fast as the machine would move and all Worm could do was watch as his mouth hung wide open.

At this point, Bows couldn't wait in the backyard for any more amount of time and made her way to the front of the house, and couldn't believe her eyes when she saw what Boulder was planning to do.

Boulder had now driven the machine across the street and onto the front lawn of the safe house. He didn't stop as he reached the front windows of the house. He just kept going, raising the scoop to window level. He was now ten feet away.

Worm noticed the windows had bars over them from the inside, but this construction machine was no match for some bars blocking the windows. Now with only five feet to go, Bows couldn't help but stare into the Boulder's wildly venomous eyes. He was obviously jacked up on the adrenaline and ready to go through any obstacle that lay ahead of him; whether that be barred up windows to the front of this safe house, or a fellow team member who he was now ready to kill.

At the moment of impact, the windows shattered and the bars crunched under the weight of the scoop, and the entire bulldozer crashed through the front of the house into the dining room. Obviously Angela heard the incredibly loud clatter of the dining room wall being torn down and knew she was in serious trouble.

"JACOBI!" she screamed.

But, she couldn't hear any response from him over the loud noises coming from the front of the house. As fast as her feet could take her, Angela ran to see what had happened and saw the giant construction machine in the living room.

There were entirely too many pieces of the house flung around, and it took her a moment to realize what was happening. She made eye contact with Boulder, and knew she was in immediate danger. A few more seconds went by before she heard Jacobi's voice loud and clear. He shouted Angela's name. He was upstairs, holding onto the staircase railing, clearly still wet from the shower, but had some pants on, as well as a white dress shirt (still unbuttoned), looking quite terrified, as he shouted, "Get to the basement!"

CHAPTER 8

TIME'S UP

I. 7 Minutes and 22 Seconds

The basement door had a lock on it, but this door wasn't like the front door. The basement door was traditional and had a regular lock and key. Angela quickly grabbed the key off the hook next to the doorframe, and unlocked the door. She flung herself into the basement and shut the door with a forceful slam. She locked the door with the key and made her way down the stairs, practically flying down the wooden steps. Her shoes weren't the most practical for running around (being dress shoes), but at least she wasn't barefoot anymore.

There was another loud reverberating explosion above her head. So loud, in fact, that this time Angela felt she was done for. The noise spooked her so badly that she ducked down and held her head in between her hands—as if that would protect her from the ceiling crashing down upon her.

But when she opened her eyes, she realized the ceiling of the basement above her was still mostly intact. A portion of it was caved in from where the bulldozer was now located, but it was still holding up. The loud booming crash must've been aftershock-destruction caused by the massive construction machine. At this point, she had reached the end of the staircase. She looked over to her right and noticed what seemed to be giant plastic containers stacked one on top of the other. She couldn't contemplate why there were so many, or what sort of objects filled them. The basement was not lit up well, so she squinted her eyes, trying to spot a good hiding place, possibly behind the stacks of containers.

Guns were fired repeatedly upstairs, and Angela practically jumped with each shot she heard. It sounded like a gang war up there and her only hope was Jacobi would find a way out.

That's when she heard the basement door being slammed into, by what seemed to be several kicks and pounding fists. Whoever these people were that wanted her dead, were right up those stairs, on the other side of the door trying to get in. It wouldn't take them long, since this door wasn't as secure as the front door. Angela slid behind one of the containers, squeezing her slim swimmer's body behind the second row. She crouched low and looked down at the basement floor, which was reflecting a soft greenish quality from what must've been a light on the other side of the basement. She peeked her head over the top container to see if she could get a better glance.

For a second, she felt like the vibrant green glow was coming from a hole in the basement wall. But then she realized what it really was, and figured out why Jacobi had sent her to the basement.

The effervescent green light wasn't coming from a hole in the wall, but from a separate room. The walls to this room were made of solid steel and could only be described as a panic room. This room was Angela's saving grace. She would be safe in this room, as long as it had a protective door that would shut behind her once inside.

At that very second, Angela straightened her body from the crouching position, she heard the door at the top of the steps rupture into countless wooden shards. Angela didn't have time to process how the door shattered like that, but it didn't matter. They were in; and the race to the panic room was on.

But there she stood. She was frozen. Fear had gotten to her head and she couldn't move any of her limbs. All Angela had to do was move the large containers out of her way, and run to the panic room before those monstrous people could get to her. It seemed so simple, but when she heard the door break and the footsteps coming down the stairs, she was stuck, standing still in her own body. The panic was sedative and for just a swift millisecond, Angela thought about what it would be like to be stabbed to death. Or shot.

It must be absolutely horrifying. Or maybe it feels like nothing at all.

Angela could see a beautiful dark woman approach the bottom of the basement steps and the frozen feeling in her body melted, because she hid behind the container as fast as her legs could bend back down into a crouching position. Of course, Bows looked for a light switch, but there was none at the bottom of the steps. She squinted her eyes, reached for her knife belted upon her right calf and held it in front of her face. It acted like a mirror to see behind her and protected her from any forward momentum attack.

"I know you're down here, bitch! So come on out and face me…woman to woman." Bows said this with quite a bit of volume in her voice, for the basement was quite large.

And there were many places a petite woman could be hiding. Bows walked left instead of right, and Angela knew she had only a few precious seconds to formulate a plan. She slowly peeked her head above the top container and unhinged the top of it. Peering inside, she saw it was filled with pet toys. Rubber balls, collars and leashes were packed inside this container. Frustratingly, this box filled of pet supplies wouldn't be of any use to Angela. Maybe if she had Jacobi's skills, she could use this junk to strangle this woman, but she knew she was no match for her and this woman's sharp knife.

Bows had found the panic room and stood in the doorway, cautious. An uneasy feeling took hold of her, standing inside this room, for she thought it could be a trap. Looking inside from the doorway, Bows had to make sure Dr. Haven wasn't in there.

She turned around, hoping Dr. Haven would be stupid enough to attack her from behind. But then she thought about her target, and recognized this woman wasn't a fellow assassin with developed skills. Dr. Angela Haven was a normal individual whom didn't have any training in combat so she was, most likely, doing what other normal individuals would be doing— hiding somewhere.

This was partially true, as Angela was hiding behind the containers, but she was also searching through them as quietly as she could. She peered into two of three of them before coming to the top container on her left side. She unhinged the lid and saw a multitude of handguns. Her eyes lit up and she grabbed the first one she could get her hands on. She heard Bows searching for her on the other side of the basement, hearing her shoes stomp on the cement basement floor.

Angela didn't know the first thing about shooting a gun. She had never even held a gun before. She was absolutely repulsed by these things, mostly because she had negative experiences being shot at. She knew enough about guns from television shows she had watched late night in her laboratory, while she and her coworkers ate bad Thai food late at night. She made sure the safety was off and held the gun with both hands.

If this bitch wants to face me woman to woman, then so be it.
But I'm bringing a gun to this knife fight.

But, Angela was shaking at the thought of having to actually pull the trigger. She didn't want to shoot this woman, even though she was endangering her life. She had never thought in a million years she'd have to shoot another human being. But this was self-defense, and she knew she had to make it to the panic room safely, to wait for Jacobi. She almost made a run for it right then and there, but then she thought she might not have to pull the trigger to this gun at all if she could distract this woman.

Opening the first container filled with the pet toys, Angela grabbed a bouncy rubber ball, and threw it as hard as she could across from her, diagonal from the panic room. The ball hit the wall with a thud and Bows heard it at once. Angela watched from across the room as Bows started making her way to that side of the basement.

Now's your chance, run!

So, she did just that. Like a wild animal, Angela knocked the containers out of her way, causing some to crash towards the ground and tumble open. She jumped over the excess components that had spilled from the open containers, and ran towards the panic room with a dominant ferocity in her steps. Dashing at full speed, Angela's adrenaline was in full throttle. Conversely, it felt like a bad dream, when your body moves in slow motion, and the monster behind you is nipping at your heels.

Bows was a master at diversions, and redirecting a target's attention from certain activities or people in her vicinity. It didn't take her long to figure out that the random noise coming from the ball Angela had thrown was just a distraction for her.

And so, when she started making her way to "examine the sound," she knew Angela was hiding in the opposite side of the basement. Once she heard the containers collapse on the floor, Bows spun around and sprinted to the panic room herself. Being only a few leaps away from Dr. Haven, Bows was now right on her tail. They both reached the proximity of the area where the green vibrant light was beaming from the doorway.

Bows was fast, but she knew Angela had a few paces on her. Bows also didn't know how rapidly the panic room door would shut, so she'd have to make a drastic move. She spun her knife in her hand so it was in a perfect position to throw, and then, without having even a second to aim, she threw the knife with her full strength right at Angela.

Angela peered over her shoulder just at that second, and noticed the deadly weapon heading straight at her. She tried to dive out of the way of the knife—but it came at her too fast and struck her left hamstring. The knife pierced her skin with ease and slid in about 3 inches deep.

Angela screamed and collapsed on the floor before reaching the panic room. There was no way she would make it to the room with the knife buried in her leg. Her fingers gripped the basement floor and with all her strength she pulled herself to the doorway of the panic room. Hand by hand, pulling herself as her leg started to bleed out. Now standing directly over her, Bows was smirking at Angela's writhing body on the ground.

Bows was enjoying the sounds of pain Dr. Haven was making and wanted to induce more agony on her. She hated Dr. Haven with a passion, and she knew this was her moment to end this horrible situation once and for all.

Bows took her left foot and slammed it down on Dr. Haven's upper thigh, causing her to yelp boisterously. Once she had most of her weight on Angela's leg, she reached for her knife and slowly pulled it out of her hamstring. Angela began to tear up and sputtered a few low sounding groans. She didn't want to cry in front of this woman, so she held in the tears as best she could—even though she was in immense pain. The blood began to pool out faster from the wound, as Bows examined the bloody knife.

"I meant to hit you square in the back but my aim was a bit off. Oh well, it still got the job done," Bows said, reaching down and flipping Angela onto her backside. "Y'all are just meaningless jobs to us. But with you…it feels a bit more personal. You caused our team to fall apart. You're the reason my boyfriend needs medical attention right now. So, when I plunge this knife into your heart, I want you to know you deserved all of this. And, most importantly, I enjoyed watching you die."

What Bows didn't realize was that Angela had the handgun tucked into the front of her pantsuit. And when Bows flipped her over, and was speaking to her, Angela had reached down and grabbed the gun, and was now pointing it at Bows chest.

"I think you have it the other way around, crazy bitch." Angela said, with a victorious glimmer in her eye.

She pulled the trigger and the gun went off, causing Bows to propel backwards dodging the bullet whizzing by her, and falling flat on her back. The gunshot was loud, and it made Angela flinch. Once Angela saw Bows lying on her back cowering, she crawled into the panic room, applying pressure to her wound with her left hand.

There was a giant black knob directly next to the entryway of the panic room on the inside and Angela reached up from the ground, wincing in pain and slammed her palm on it. The room's steel door slid shut and sealed itself with a locking mechanism that reminded Angela of a space station door. No one was going to get in this room now. Once the door was sealed shut, the green vibrant light switched off, and the white glow of fluorescent light bulbs lit the little room up.

Her eyes darted around the room and she spotted a red box marked, 'Medical' and opened it at once. Angela unwrapped the bandages inside and did her best to sew up the bloody stab wound. Her hands were trembling, so it was no easy undertaking; however, the adrenaline was pumping in her veins, keeping her focused. After a couple minutes of sewing up her wound and bandaging it, she looked up and noticed a small television screen next to the medical box. She turned the power button on and could immediately see the foyer of the house. It looked completely disheveled. Flipping through the many camera feed options, she finally found Jacobi.

The camera feed was coming from the backyard of the house. At first, she couldn't tell who it was, but then she knew without any hesitation it was Jacobi's body—sprawled out on the grass looking as lifeless as can be. He was on his back, arms crisscrossed over his head, unconscious, or worse yet, dead.

II. 8 Minutes and 22 Seconds Ago

The mirror was foggy from the steamy shower, so Jacobi couldn't see his reflection too clearly. His slasher-horror flick red marks stood out (due to all his minor cuts and bruises), in the blurry reflection, as well as his broad silhouette. His blurred body mirrored a ghostly image of his actual self. Using his bruised right hand, he wiped the mirror so he could see his face properly. Staring back at him, were his light blue tired eyes. All he needed was a quick catnap, or at least a strong cup of coffee, and he would be energized again.

He touched the spot on his head where the boat explosion had knocked him out and cut a shallow gash in the back of his head. He definitely needed stitches, but a butterfly stitch would have to do for now. He grabbed the medical kit in the bathroom and applied it on the back of his head. It wasn't bleeding anymore, but that didn't mean it couldn't open up again.

After dressing in his fresh pristine white collared shirt and black dress pants from the closet, he decided to choose between two different ties to put on. The first being a light green color, reminding him of Angela's eyes, and the second being a striped blue and gray, reminding him of an uptight politician. He held each one up against his bare chest, delaying buttoning his shirt until he was completely dry. He came upon a decision; he couldn't help but be drawn to the mint-green option, as he threw each of the ties upon the bed in front of him. His shoes looked freshly polished as he slipped each one on, tying them tight and finally feeling like himself once again.

Jacobi heard the destructive thunderous sound of the living room wall collapsing from downstairs. Without wasting a millisecond Jacobi got into full-on protector mode and sprinted to the closet. He knew this was where there was some weaponry, so he reached for the top shelf to grab a grenade, which was kept in case of an emergency just like this.

He ran from the closet to the bed again and reached under the bed frame to detach a handgun—much like the one he had previously, before it was lost in the ocean.

"JACOBI!" Angela's scream was almost inaudible because of all the crashing noises happening downstairs. But, Jacobi could still make it out. They were separated, but if he could just get her to the basement panic room in time, she'd be safe.

Jacobi sprinted from the main bedroom to the top of the staircase. Once there, he could see the giant bulldozer in the middle of the living room. There were too many pieces of debris, shattered glass and dry wall dust to make out the driver of the machine, but he could see Angela's stunned face below him in the foyer.

"ANGELA! Get to the basement!" Jacobi shouted, grabbing her attention.

It all happened so fast, but before the smoke cleared, Angela had opened the basement door and shut it behind her. The only thing that mattered now was getting Angela into the panic room.

A smaller petite woman ran to the basement door from the living room and Jacobi recognized her from earlier in the day. The bows in her hair sparked his memory. He had seen this woman on the beach with her associate -the same one who had shot Mr. Hicks. They had made eye contact on the beach, and Jacobi knew then she was apart of the operation in some way. Now, it all came together. She was a fellow assassin, a part of this deranged team that was hell-bent on taking out Angela.

Acting without hesitation, Jacobi took the pin out of the grenade and whipped it unswervingly toward the bulldozer. It clanked against the front of the scoop and Jacobi watched the man driving it dive out the window into the front lawn as the grenade exploded with a furious boom. The dining room floor shook with a terrible force, causing it to partially cave in, underneath the weight of the bulldozer.

It held up for the most part, but the dining room was now in complete ruins. This was the perfect opportunity for Jacobi to gain the upper hand. Creeping down the staircase one by one with his gun pointed directly in front of his chest, he made sure to keep his (now wide-awake) eyes alert, making sure to look for either assassin. Bows had made her way to the living room when the grenade exploded. But, she was back to banging on the basement door with her fists and high kicks. That's when Boulder came rushing back into the house, with barely a scratch on him from the explosion. He was lucky the part of the wall that wasn't caved in blocked the explosion from injuring him too much.

In a manic act, Boulder began shooting in Jacobi's vicinity, screaming at the top of his lungs like a deranged cave man. His face was covered in white smoky debris and bullets were flying about Jacobi's feet. A retreat up the stairs was his only move at this point, which gave Bows the perfect opportunity to place the device Worm had given her outside, and turn the contraption counter-clockwise. Three red lights lit up and then the basement door exploded. Shattered splinters of the wooden door were flown apart the foyer.

Bows ducked out of the way, but she was still hit by a few pieces of the door. But, at least she was in. She made her way down the basement steps taking a careful approach, as she was the only one of her team members ready to corner the target.

The gunshots were loud and plenty. Boulder opted not to wear a bullet-proof vest—even though Worm told him it might be beneficial—because he wanted full range of movement. He didn't want anything slowing him down, as he wasn't that quick to begin with, due to his large stature. He made his way up the stairs firing off shots left and right with his guns. Jacobi was backpedaling as he was shooting in Boulder's general direction, but neither man made contact as they didn't have a sturdy footing.

Jacobi dove into the extra bedroom, right as Boulder made his way to the top of the stairs. The gun Jacobi was using had less than a couple of bullets left in the clip, which wouldn't be enough to stop this oncoming attack. He looked around the room and remembered the gun stashed in the plant soil, reaching into the dirt and pulling it out, just in the knick of time. Boulder stepped into the doorframe, ready to shoot Jacobi in the head, when Jacobi fired off the gun from the plant. Jacobi had an open shot and hit Boulder square in his right rib cage. The bullet didn't go through Boulder, but bounced off his rib bone, causing immense pain, but barely a flesh wound.

Now it was time for Boulder to retreat, so he ran down the long hallway towards the master bedroom. But Jacobi was a good enough shot to try to shoot through the bedroom wall. He fired off several shots, in a single horizontal line, each just a few inches from Boulders large tree trunk legs, catapulting him into the master bedroom.

Jacobi did his signature kick-up flip to get back onto his feet, and slid through the doorway, guns in front of his body aimed at the master bedroom. The door had slammed shut, but this didn't stop an adrenaline fueled Jacobi run full throttle towards the bedroom door, smashing it wide open with a bang.

Boulder was ready for Jacobi, knowing he would be reckless enough to follow him right away. He had just enough time to get his knife into his hand and stand close to the doorframe waiting for his adversary. Boulder held the knife in his right hand and came down upon Jacobi with a robust plunge.

Luckily for Jacobi, he had enough momentum crashing through the door that Boulder missed his first attempt at stabbing him. The knife missed his body by a few inches, hitting the carpeted floor with a dull thud. Jacobi didn't have enough reaction time to dodge the next attack though, as Boulder swung his right arm around and sliced Jacobi's rear deltoid shoulder blade. It was a deep slice, but Jacobi could barely feel the sting.

Boulder had a better advantage from this angle, so Jacobi dove into a somersaulted roll beside the bed, landing on his back. This caused Boulder to smile because he knew he had the upper hand in the fight. He could finish this menace off once and for all. But this was also Boulder's main fault in hand-to-hand combat: his inflated ego.

He had thought he had already won this battle, so he took just a millisecond too long to strike again, and when he leaned over Jacobi to plunge his knife down into his chest, Jacobi remembered his martial arts training and lifted his legs up and kicked with all his might.

Hitting Boulder straight in the chest, Jacobi caused Boulder to propel back into the wall with a mighty force. His body slammed into the wall hard, causing him to drop his knife and hit his head. Seeing spots, Boulder tried to gain his composure, but wasn't fast enough for Jacobi's quick speed.

By the time Boulder managed to get back on his feet, Jacobi had enough time to grab the light green tie on the bed and come around Boulder from behind using the tie as a strangulation weapon. Jacobi wrapped the tie around Boulder's large neck, and gripped the ends tight with his fists. His hands were bloodied and slippery but he didn't let the tie slip out of his hand, even as Boulder tried to smash Jacobi into the wall to break his grasp.

Due to his side wound from the gunshot, Boulder's strength—which he always depended on for a fight—was at a low. Blood was draining from his body, slowly but steadily. He needed to act fast or he was going to be choked out and killed. He still had immense lower body strength, even if his windpipe was being suppressed for the time being.

He practically carried himself and Jacobi's weight to the opposite side of the room and spun his body around with the last bit of breath in his lungs. Jacobi clung to the tie with both fists, but couldn't control where the rest of his body flung. Boulder had noticed the full-length mirror across the room and executed his last ditch plan perfectly.

Jacobi's body was flung into the mirror like a rag-doll, causing him to release his grip on the tie. Both men were now slumped over on the floor, bloodied and bruised even more than before. They managed to catch their breath but weren't moving much. They had each depleted their endurance levels, being quite equal in their hand-to-hand combat skills.

Boulder was the first to get to his knees, still coughing and trying to take a breath that didn't feel like choking on sand. He wanted nothing more than to step over Jacobi and break his neck with his bare hands, but he just couldn't find the energy to get to his feet. They had made eye contact at this point and Jacobi was completely wiped out.

Jacobi, now leaning against the broken mirror, noticed a large piece of the shattered mirror by his left hand. Before Boulder could get to his feet, he grabbed the piece of jagged glass quickly and swiped the piece of mirror as hard as he could right over Boulder's right eye.

It was a direct hit and Boulder's eye was now cut open. Blood poured from his eye socket, as he put his hands over his face, falling backwards and onto the floor. Both men were hurt badly. Cut up and already swollen from the major hits they had each taken, they managed to gain some sort of possession of their bodies and, one by one, made their way back to their feet.

Swaying back and forth, Jacobi gripped onto the wall behind him; dizzy from being flung into the mirror. He had shattered pieces of glass stuck in his back and hamstrings, and crooked lines of blood smeared across the wall behind him. Boulder was still holding onto his eye, when he spotted the other tie on the bed. He grabbed it and tied it around his head to keep pressure on the bloody eye socket. With his good eye, he spotted Jacobi falling towards the master bedroom balcony doors and ran full speed at him, tackling his opponent into the glass doors.

Understandably, they both knew this was a fight to the death, as they crashed through the glass doors onto the balcony. The balcony wasn't very large; it had a single lawn chair upon it and a small gas grill. It was a new addition to the safe house; a decision Jacobi didn't understand when his boss had built it, off the master bedroom last summer. He didn't fight it, because Mr. Hornsby told him the door would be barred off just like every other window to the safe house.

Unfortunately, Mr. Hornsby didn't complete this task, and now, Jacobi and Boulder had crashed through the door and onto this balcony. Since Boulder used Jacobi's body as a shield when they had crashed through, he had the upper hand once again and picked Jacobi up with his shaking hands and punched him square in the jaw.

This jarring hit caused Jacobi to become disoriented. He was attempting to grasp onto the railing of the balcony when Boulder used all his might and flipped him over the railing. In one final attempt to hold on, Jacobi clung onto the edge of the balcony with his bloody fingers.

The two men looked each other in the eyes (or eye from Boulder's point of view) one more time before Jacobi's grip slipped. His fingers betrayed his body and he let go of the edge, falling from the balcony to the grass below him. Unconscious from the fall, Jacobi lay there like a dead body. Boulder squinted his left eye trying to grip the railing tight. He was dizzy and saw two of everything. He stumbled back into the bedroom crushing the glass and mirror fragments under his shoes and found Jacobi's gun beside the doorframe. He grabbed it off the floor, now holding onto his injured bleeding rib cage and staggered back to the balcony looking down at the man he was about to kill.

Boulder held the gun out and pointed it down at Jacobi's body—or at least one of Jacobi's bodies that he was seeing at the moment. His index finger pulled the trigger back ever so slightly, and that's when he saw the spots again. The last thing Boulder saw was the blue sky above him, collapsing onto his back, and passing out. The impact of the fight he had experienced with Jacobi had gotten the best of him as well. The two opponents were both unconscious and left for dead.

This was the precise moment Angela switched the panic room television on and saw Jacobi sprawled out on the grass looking lifeless as can be. On his back, arms crisscrossed over his head, lying there without any movement.

III. Late for a Very Important Date

Angela put her hands over her mouth in disbelief. Her knight in shining armor was lying in the grass, bloody and immobile. Hating herself for even thinking it, she couldn't help but ponder if Jacobi was dead, or alive.

He can't be dead. Not now. Not after...everything.

She flipped the channels to every camera feed on the premises and found the large man who drove the construction machine through the front of the house. He was in the same condition Jacobi was—laying on his back, bloody and lifeless. From what she could tell, he was in the master bedroom.

She flipped through the other camera feeds and came to the basement camera. There was a wide-eyed lens camera above the panic room door, but the basement was obstructed by Bows' face. She was right up against the lens as she pulled the camera right off the wall, smashing it on the floor.

Leaning against the panic room wall, Angela was now blind to the perpetrator outside the panic room door. This room was not only impenetrable as rooms go, but it was also sound proof. So when Angela couldn't take her frustration and anxiety anymore, she belted out a long roaring scream at the top of her lungs. She felt so hopeless.

No tears came out of her eyes, as she had shed a majority of them just a short while ago thinking about Mr. Hicks being shot and killed earlier in the day. As well as thinking about her ex-fiancé, Jeremy. She pulled the picture of the two of them out from her pants pocket and stared at it.

I hope you're happy, Jeremy. And if I die today, I don't blame you. For anything.

While Angela was reminiscing about her past relationship, Worm had snuck down the basement stairs. He had walked through the front door, after his contraption had finally reached 100 percent; though he could've walked right into the house through the giant hole in the dining room just as easily.

He heard way too many gunshots and breaking noises to come into the house at that point. Once the pandemonium settled down, he had radioed his team members but only Bows answered, letting him know she was in the basement and to bring more of his nifty contraptions.

"A panic room? Holy shit. Wasn't expecting this." Worm muttered touching the door as if it were made of an alien metal he had never encountered before.

"Can you get the door open or not?" Bows asked, frustrated and tapping her fingernails on the metal.

"This is going to call for some light calibrations to my device. Be patient with me."

Bows rolled her eyes clearly wanting Worm to see her annoyed. All she wanted was to get inside this room and kill their target so this nightmare of a day could end. She didn't know what was going to happen with her team, but she couldn't care less at this point. She just wanted Rocky to be healthy and by her side. That's all she needed.

"I'm going to call Duke while you work on this thing. The faster, the better, Worm."

Worm mimicked her by mouthing her words back to her in a childlike impersonation. He hated the way she spoke to him. He actually hated the way the whole team spoke to him, except for Ace. They had the strongest bond because Ace treated him like an intelligent individual who brought something unique and valid to the team. The longer Ace was away, the more Worm thought about leaving this team. The money was beginning to seem not worth the verbal abuse he had to put up with from the team members and the danger he was constantly in.

Bows radioed for Boulder, but there was no answer. She was getting worried, even though she was quite confident he could hold his own against that prick of a bodyguard. But Boulder usually had his brother's backup in situations like these. Bows figured she would look for Boulder as soon as she had called Duke, and informed him of the team's situation.

"Duke? I can't hear you that well. Are you there?"

"I said hello Bows…"

Bows could now hear his voice, but it wasn't Duke. It was Ace.

"Ace?"

"It's me. Thanks for the knife. Really helped me out there."

"What did you do to Duke?"

"He's fine. A bit cut up, but he'll survive. If I don't kill him after all of this, that is."

"You know why I helped you, right? This doesn't mean I'm on your side. We are still killing her. I just didn't want you in the same predicament. Even if I do have strong hateful feelings towards you right now."

"I promise, if you touch a hair on her head, Bows—I'll—"

"You'll what? Kill me? Try me, asshole. This mission is getting done. Not because we were already paid. Screw the money. Not because we haven't failed a mission yet. Screw our perfect record as a team. I'm doing it for Rocky."

"So, you and Rocky get to be together because you took Pure and fell in love, but that's not reason enough to end this mission for me? I don't get to be with my true love?"

"Don't say his name. He might not live because of all of this nonsense."

"See—that's the difference between you and I. You see this as nonsense, whereas I see this all happening for a reason."

"Is that what your faith is telling you? Oh, please. Spare me that mumbo jumbo bullshit."

"I'll be at the safe house in no time, Bows. Get the hell away from there, or else…"

"Screw yourself, Ace."

CLICK. <DIAL TONE>

Bows hung up on Ace and exhaled deeply. She knew he wasn't going to hold back anymore. She could hear it in his voice. This meant everything to Ace, and if the team were still at the safe house by the time he arrived, it'd be trouble for everyone.

"It's working, Bows. It's just a matter of minutes before this baby opens up for us," Worm said, delightfully.

"Great, now go look for Boulder. We need to get the hell out of here. I'll take her out when the door opens. I need you to find Boulder and tell him Ace is on his way here."

"But, how did—"

"Worm! Just go."

Worm scoffed and begrudgingly made his way to the basement staircase going up the stairs lazily. He wanted to be there when the panic room door opened, but Bows was right. If Ace was actually on his way, he didn't want to be anywhere near him.

Searching every room in the downstairs floor, Worm knew Boulder had to be upstairs. He called up the staircase for him, but there was no answer. Worm wasn't exactly a field agent, so he didn't have weaponry training or anything of that sort. He was strictly on the team for his intelligence in computer hacking and gadgetry.

Walking ever so slowly, he finally made his way to the master bedroom where he saw Boulder laying on his back unconscious by the balcony door. Worm tried his best to step around the broken pieces of mirror and glass but the crunching noises under his shoes were inevitable. Worm checked Boulder's pulse and he was still alive.

"Boulder, man. Wake up! Boulder, we have to go!" Worm shook Boulder and that's when he noticed he had been shot in the side. The bullet wound didn't look deep, but if this wound wasn't taken care of shortly, Boulder would inevitably bleed out and die. Worm radioed Bows letting her know Boulder was hurt and he needed her help to carry him down the stairs.

"Just a minute, Worm. 3...2...1..."

The device blinked three green lights with a clicking noise and the panic room door slid open. Bows expected to find Dr. Haven crouching in a corner arms around her knees crying, but she didn't see that. She saw an empty room.

Where the hell is this bitch?

And then she saw it. There was a hidden latch on the floor of the room. A door that popped open unveiled a ladder down to a dark tunnel.

Of course.

Bows wanted to go down the ladder and through the tunnel to chase Dr. Haven. And she would have, if Worm didn't desperately need her assistance to save Boulder's life. Before she stepped out of the panic room, she spotted a piece of paper beside the hidden door. Dr. Haven must've dropped it while escaping.

It was a picture of Dr. Haven and another man. They looked like lovers in this picture.

Hmm, this might come in handy.

"I'll be right up, Worm. But, I have a random question for you. You know that facial recognition program you created—how well does that work?"

CHAPTER 9

SHADOWS

I. The Twilight Hour

Dried blood had stained his shirt and coat from the cut on the side of his skull that was still slowly dripping down his neck. The cut wasn't deep, but the aching pain from the pistol whip hurt like a bitch. As the grogginess lifted from his tender head, he wondered how long he had been unconscious. Duke remembered being at Ace's mercy against the wall, and then there was just blackness.

The rope Ace had tied around Duke's hands was still wrapped tight around his wrists. But as he struggled to get his hands loose, he thought about all the times he had been in a situation just like this and, somehow, managed to get free. He tried to twist and turn his body to release some of the pressure from his wrists, but all that did was remind him of his shoulder being stabbed by a sharp pocketknife.

It had been a while since Duke had been in the field. These days he sat comfortably behind his desk at *Sway*, letting his team do the dirty work. It was a profitable job - being the man behind the missions—and much less dangerous. Maybe it was from the adrenaline he was feeling, or maybe he was still a bit out of it, but Duke began to chuckle at the state he was in. He would have never imagined being in this dusty mausoleum, tied up and stabbed.

The chair he was sitting upon was made of wood, and his feet weren't tied to the chair so Duke did the only thing he could think of and jumped up to his feet, swinging the chair behind him into the tomb. The legs broke off and the chair fell apart rather easily. His wrists were still bound behind him, but at least he was now mobile. He was a middle-aged man, but he still had the flexibility to get his hands in front of his body.

Now, all he had to do was call Boulder or Bows to come pick him up, but alas, his cellphone was gone.

Damn you, Ace.

There was a lamp inside the mausoleum, with a dimly lit light bulb giving off just enough light for Duke to see a few feet in front of him. The dim light was casting a large shadow of Duke's hunched over silhouette. He was still in immense pain from his stab wound and from being pistol-whipped. Duke glanced at his shadow and then looked at the lamp. Noticing the sharp edges of the iron lamp, he used them to cut himself free from the rope, suffering through the shoulder pain.

He walked outside and was happy to breathe some fresh air. Being a bit disoriented, he spun around in a small circle while his eyes adjusted to the setting sun. He walked the half-mile out of the cemetery and into the gravel parking lot next to the singular funeral home on the property.

An elderly couple was leaning against one of the only cars in the parking lot embracing each other, as the woman cried into the man's shoulder. Obviously, they had just visited someone's grave that was close to them. Most people would see this couple and feel some sort of empathy, but not Duke. He saw an easy opportunity.

Sneaking up on them and without any warning, Duke said, "I like your hat, mister."

"Excuse me?" The elderly man asked, not expecting to get a compliment on his fedora.

"I said I like your hat." And when Duke was close enough to the couple, he pulled them apart from one another and put the elderly woman in a chokehold position. The elderly gentleman—her husband—shouted out for help trying to get this man away from his wife. But Duke was a ruthless man, and shoved the older man to the ground. He told the couple neither of them would get hurt if they gave him their car keys.

A minute later, Duke was driving out of the cemetery in their car. He looked in the rearview mirror at the two bodies laying on the gravel parking lot. He didn't have to do it, but he had to take his anger out somehow. There were now two additional bodies lying in this cemetery.

It didn't take long for Duke to drive back to *Sway*, where Rocky was recovering from his gunshot wound. He had been put on a morphine drip and lots of pain medication, but hadn't been awake since earlier in the day. He was lucky the bullet went right through him and didn't hit his lung or any other vital organs. However, Rocky wouldn't be doing any chest workouts for a long time.

Duke made his way to the secret elevator in his office and down into the hidden headquarters. This is where Rocky was resting, on one of the cots laid out for him.

While driving from the cemetery back to *Sway*, Duke had time to think of his next move. He knew he had to take things up a notch if he was going to keep his team members alive and complete this mission. His plan included Rocky's help, even if Dr. Peterson advised him not to wake him. He had also advised Duke that Rocky was in no condition to go back in the field after a serious gunshot wound like the one he had experienced. But this advice didn't change Duke's mind. He knew he would have to make due with Rocky not being one hundred percent because he was running out of options.

Dr. Peterson was told to leave *Sway* after Duke wrote him a check for his medical assistance and discreetness. After Dr. Peterson had left the club, Duke took over as Rocky's doctor. He didn't mess around with drugs he didn't understand, but he did know a thing or two about opiates (being an addict for much of his life) and how they numbed the physicality of body pains. He concocted a serum strong enough to wake Rocky.

In a matter of minutes, Rocky woke up feeling confused, but oddly alert. He struggled to sit but with Duke's help he sat up, looking down at his bandaged upper chest. The pain was numbed by whatever cocktail medication Duke had shot him up with.

"You're alive, Rocky. You have some healing to do, but unfortunately there isn't time for that right now. You're going to have to be strong for the team right now."

"I don't understand. What happened?" Rocky asked, feeling quite confused about the whole situation.

"I'll fill you in on everything I know, but we have to move fast. Phase two needs to commence right away."

"I'll do whatever I have to, especially if that means killing that son of a bitch, Ace. Or the asshole that shot me. I mean what the hell happened? Is Ace in cahoots with that bodyguard and our target?"

"I know you have questions, and I'll explain all I know on the way."

"On the way to where? And what's phase two?" Rocky asked, trying to stand up. He was definitely in no physical shape to be doing anything but resting, but he was stubborn and wanted to help his team. He would be ready for anything, with the help of some strong drugs.

Duke explained to Rocky they'd be going on a field trip to the house of Dr. Haven's boss, Dr. William Rayne. It was time to get personal with Dr. Haven. She seemed like a good person. And what kind of good person wouldn't try to save the life of a close friend?

Duke gave Rocky a few pills to take along with a shot of opiates and Rocky felt like he was a new man. He could barely feel the sting of the gunshot wound, although the drugs were taking their toll on his mind. He seemed a bit out of it, but Duke thought this tradeoff was well worth it, considering he didn't value Rocky's mind—but his physical abilities.

Before they left, Duke made sure to grab an earpiece communication device and channeled it to Rocky's. He helped him walk out of the hidden headquarters and up the elevator. The two assassins left *Sway* and walked towards the car Duke had stolen. The sun had set beyond the horizon, and the sky was colored with a brilliant reddish glow. There was just enough remaining sunlight to cast a shadow over Rocky's face, as he laid low in the backseat of the car.

Rocky daydreamed of his revenge on Ace—as well as the bodyguard who had shot him on the beach. He thought about the countless ways he could hurt each of them for spinning his life out of control. He smiled at the bloody thoughts in his head.

Bows also came to mind. He thought about her beautiful face, her gentle cascading voice and how badly he wanted to kiss her neck, as that was her tender sweet spot. He couldn't imagine what life was like before he took Pure and looked into Bows' eyes. The two of them were meant for each other and, in a way, he had Dr. Haven to thank for that. He was grateful for the love drug she created, but he was also adamant about finishing the mission, regardless of how grateful he was to this arbitrary doctor. And now, Duke and Rocky were onto phase two of this mission, and nothing was going to get in their way.

II. Our Former Selves

Dead. That's how Jacobi felt coming to on the grassy lawn of the safe house. He opened his eyes looking at the dazzling reddish sky above him. He shut his eyes again, not wanting to feel all the pain his body felt, hoping this was some sort of nightmare he could awaken from. But alas, this was reality. He didn't know it at the time, but he had a concussion from hitting his head hard on the ground when he had fallen off the balcony.

Bloody and bruised didn't even cover how bad he looked and felt. Reopening his eyes, he observed the sky looked much darker from the reddish hue that he just witnessed. He must've passed out for a bit since he first opened his eyes. Not knowing if any of his bones were broken right away, he moved as slowly as he could, moving his right arm from over his head, to his side. He knew just from this slow movement that he had messed up his back in some fashion. It didn't feel broken, but it hurt with a throbbing ache.

Moving his neck was definitely a chore, looking down at his feet, and noticing how shiny his dress shoes looked. He wiggled his toes and was relieved he could do that simple task. At least his spinal cord wasn't broken, or his legs for that matter. And then he tried to move his left arm, but couldn't. Something was definitely wrong. He looked over at his shoulder and saw that it was completely dislocated from its socket.

Sitting up as slowly as his aching back could go, Jacobi took three deep breaths and tried to place his shoulder back where it should have been. But it wasn't as easy as he had hoped and needed more support than just a pull from his other arm. Somehow managing to get to his sore feet, he walked to the back of the house and leaned his left arm against the wall and slammed his shoulder back into the socket. It popped in with a cracking noise, and he yelped out with a shallow exhale.

Jacobi's shoulder was the worst of the many painful injuries on his body, but he was also limping from some sort of injury to his hip as well. He was cut up and his head hurt worse than any tequila hangover he'd ever have before.

Once he got himself together, he walked around the front of the safe house and into the destroyed dining room without a front wall. The damage done to this house looked unfixable as the floor had almost caved in. Taking his time, he carefully maneuvered his way out of this room and into the foyer, keeping his eyes open for any sign of the assassins that had attacked him and Angela. Jacobi didn't have any weapons on him and if one of them tried to attack him at this moment, they would, without a doubt, kill him quite easily.

But this fact didn't stop him from walking into the house unarmed, as he knew he had to get to Angela. He walked over the broken shards of the wooden basement door that had exploded and down the stairs holding onto the railing like an elderly person that was recovering from hip replacement surgery.

He made his way to the bottom of the stairs and was worried as soon as he saw the green glow from the panic room. This meant the door wasn't sealed and either Angela hadn't made it inside, or she did and she found the entrance to the tunnel. He looked inside the room and noticed the hatch had been opened.

Thank god you found it, Angela. I'll meet you, soon.

Relieved that he had proof Angela was still alive, Jacobi wasn't as reckless as he had been when reentering the safe house. He searched the lower level of the house for the assassins but there was no sign of them. He had to stay alive for Angela, and needed to defend himself if the assassins were still here. He went directly to the kitchen and grabbed the largest knife he could find. Making his way through every room on the lower floor, he knew if they were still in this house, they'd have to be upstairs.

Each step up the stairs was a bit of a chore for Jacobi's body. He was in rough shape from the fight and the fall. With each step he took, a different thought racked his mind.

What if the assassins followed Angela through the secret hatch and down the tunnel? Maybe she's not alive. No, she has to be. But where are they if they didn't follow her?

Making sure to check every room in the upstairs level, he left no corner unchecked. There was no sign of the assassins, except for the bloody mess left from the brutal fight that occurred in the master bedroom. Pieces of the broken glass crunched under Jacobi's slick dress shoes. Picking up the bloody light green tie off the floor, he walked into the master bathroom, turned the light on and took off his already unbuttoned dress shirt. It was a pristine white just a little while ago, and now it was covered in dried blood streaks.

He placed the tie and the kitchen knife on the sink and found the medical kit stashed under the sink. Before he began to sew himself up with a needle and thread, he grabbed Angela's cell phone from her beach bag (where she had put it after her phone call to her parents) and put the phone in his pants pocket. He wanted her to have it when he met up with her just in case they were to separate again.

The house was eerily silent. There were no dogs barking outside and no commotion anywhere in the safe house. The sun had set just a little bit ago and the darkness was beginning to creep into this empty house. Jacobi knew he was alone here, safe for the time being, but he needed to meet up with Angela as soon as possible—especially if the assassins were still after her.

As he was applying the antiseptic lotion to his cuts and bandaging them as fast as he could, he heard a single piece of glass being compressed by someone's shoe. The sound came from the bedroom just a few steps from the adjoining bathroom he was standing in. Without making a sound, Jacobi picked up the kitchen knife from the countertop and held it at eye level in front of him. The bathroom door slightly cracked open, so Jacobi cautiously stepped behind it, trying to peek through the crack of the doorway.

There hadn't been any other noises of glass cracking since he heard the first piece, but he knew whoever stepped on it, was still out there, making sure not to move again. Sweat was forming on Jacobi's brow, as the temperature was still quite high outside, and in the house. Jacobi's grip on the knife was tight in his left hand—since his right arm was still pretty impaired—and he was ready to attack if necessary, even in his wounded state.

There it was again, another crunch of the glass under a foot from outside the bathroom door. This time, there was no pausing afterwards. The person outside the bathroom knew someone was here and they wanted Jacobi to know they were waiting for him.

"I know you're in there. I'm not going to hurt you, but you need to come out so we can have ourselves a chat."

Jacobi had no clue who this mystery man could be, but he knew damn well what a 'chat' entailed from an assassin's point of view. And if this man was another assassin, there would be another fight; but this time Jacobi wasn't evenly matched due to his beat up body. If the man was anything in stature like the previous assassin he had just fought, he was surely in trouble.

"Honestly, man, I just want to speak with you. I feel like—"

WHAM!

Jacobi kicked the bathroom door wide open, hitting the man square in the face, knocking him back a few paces. The man was dressed all in black, quite handsome and had a gold cross around his neck. Jacobi held the kitchen knife close in front of his right shoulder, ready to attack.

"Whoa! Keep it civil! I don't want to hurt you. I know you're one of Dr. Haven's bodyguards. I need to see her."

"So you can kill her? You're one of them—one of the assassins after her, aren't you?" Jacobi was shouting, demanding answers.

He was now standing over Ace, ready to plunge the knife into his chest.

"The name's Ace. And, I don't want to kill her. I want to save her."

III. 7-3-3-0

Angela had made her way through the dark tunnel that smelled like a sewer. In fact, for all intents and purposes, this tunnel was a sewer. There was a small stream of dirty water passing through that she tried to avoid stepping in, but it was unavoidable. This was the type of water Angela wasn't fond of.

Trudging on down the tunnel, she wondered how long it could possibly be and where she would end up. There were a few twists and turns, but for the most part, it was just one long tube of darkness. She had left her cellphone in the safe house, so there was no flashlight app to help her see. That also meant there was no way she could contact Jacobi. They had exchanged numbers when they had stayed the night in the hotel.

But even if she could contact Jacobi, it didn't mean he would answer. Last she saw him, he was lying on the grass looking dead as could be. She wanted to come to his aid, but there was no way out of the panic room but down the ladder and into this tunnel.

When she finally reached the end of the tunnel, there was another ladder leading up to another hatch. But this hatch had a code lock on it. One could only open the hatch from the inside with the code—therefore removing any possibility of someone coming through this hatch and into the panic room from the other side. The code was written on a piece of paper inside an envelope that was duct taped to the hatch.

7-3-3-0 #

Angela put the piece of paper back into the envelope and taped it back to the hatch.

This code better be right. I'm done with this tunnel.

Typing the code in the code lock, the hatch unlatched, and Angela pushed it open. Without any hesitation, she popped her head up and looked up at three individuals wearing all black. At first, she thought she was a dead woman. The assassins were smarter than her and were waiting for her to come up and out of the tunnel. But then her eyes adjusted to the bright lights coming from the fluorescent lighting in this room and she noticed they were all wearing aprons.

Looking around the room the hatch door was in the center of, Angela decided to climbed out and see where she had arrived. It was a kitchen full of coffee makers and whizzing machines. There was a label on one of the coffee cups she saw in the sink labeled, Hornsby's Coffee House.

The three baristas had stunned looks on their faces as they had no idea the metal looking square on the kitchen floor was a hatch to a secret tunnel leading to a panic room inside a safe house for Mr. Hornsby's bodyguards and their charges. One of the baristas dropped her coffee cup in shock when Angela stepped out of the hatch and onto the floor.

"Uhh...what the?" the barista with a mullet haircut muttered.

"I was just looking for the bathroom. Must've gotten lost. Excuse me," Angela said, not knowing what to say. "I'll just be going back to my seat now. But, I could definitely go for a cup of your strongest coffee."

Angela figured why not take a load off as she waited for Jacobi to meet her at this random coffee shop. He had to know where the tunnel led. That was, if he was still breathing. If not, she'd stay here until they closed and then she'd make a decision of what to do next.

IV. Hit and Run

"I don't know why, but I think I'm actually starting to believe you, Mr. Ace. Your story seems legit, it's just hard to trust someone that's apart of a team that keeps trying to end my life," Jacobi said. "So, forgive the precautions I'm taking with you."

They were walking down the staircase, Ace in front of Jacobi, holding his hands up above his head. Ace wanted to speak to Jacobi without turning around to face him.

"It's understandable. And it's just, Ace. No 'mister' necessary. I know you must think my story is crazy, but it's true. I want nothing more than Dr. Haven to be safe and protected from my team. Well, my *ex-team* now."

Normally, Ace would never have his back to a stranger like this, but he had no choice if he wanted Jacobi to believe in him. He had to give him some leverage at this point. They reached the bottom of the staircase and Ace looked around the foyer, still hands above his head, fingers interlocked.

"Just through this room, Ace."

"Let me guess, the same brut that fought you also drove this bulldozer through the house too, right?"

"You'd be correct in that assumption."

"For the record, he's a class-A asshole."

Stepping around the chaos that was the dining room, Ace placed his feet around the semi-caved in floor that was barely holding up by shreds of wood and plaster. The grenade really took a toll on the dining room's foundation, especially with the weight of the bulldozer upon it.

"You know, I'd have to agree with you there. I hate that prick," Jacobi said, stepping around the fragmented pieces of the floorboards.

"Can I just tell you, I really appreciate you believing me in this insane situation. I tried to communicate all of this to the rest of my team and they couldn't even—"

Ace had no time to react. Jacobi shoved Ace with all his might into the front of the bulldozer and onto the fragile collapsible floor. With the sudden added force of Ace's body weight, the floor had no chance of staying intact and down went the bulldozer, along with Ace through the disintegrating floor.

Ace didn't even have time to shout more than a "Fuuu—," which Jacobi couldn't even hear because it was all but silenced by the deafening sounds of the collapse. The bulldozer hit the basement floor hard, along with the dining room sofa and the rest of the damaged floor. Jacobi looked down into the large open hole that now looked down into the basement and saw Ace, face down under the couch, but out of the way of the bulldozer. Ace couldn't know for sure, but he didn't look dead from the fall. He was most likely just unconscious from the fall.

Either way, Jacobi would've been fine with the result. He didn't believe a word Ace had told him about taking Pure and falling in love with Angela. It was all too farfetched and seemed like the perfect ploy to get close enough to kill her. All that Jacobi was concerned about was getting to Angela. He was praying she would be at Hornsby's Coffee House. That's where the tunnel led. That's where he was on his way to.

Unfortunately, the motorcycle he had stolen from the man at the ice cream shop was now gone. One of the assassins must've taken it as they fled the safe house. Jacobi had no choice but to hot wire one of the neighbor's cars a few houses over. He briefly thought about whose car he was stealing—some random mother with two kids that was already late for her Pilates class, coming out onto her driveway and trying to figure out what happened to her car. And then he snickered, thinking her day wasn't half as bad as his had already been.

Angela was now on her third cup of cappuccino and was buzzing from the caffeine. At this point, the sky was a deep velvety purple and dark blues. There were no more shadows cast from the sunlight, just an overall darkness from the night sky. Angela was getting restless as she looked out the front window and knew the coffee house would be closing in a few minutes. She brushed the golden locks away from her eyes and bit her lip, almost on the verge of having a mild panic attack, not knowing what was to come next. But, that's when she heard the sound of tires squealing in front of the coffee house.

The black SUV pulled right into the first spot, and a beat up Jacobi stepped out of the front door, still not moving his left arm. They made eye contact through the front window and the anxiety melted from each of their bodies. Angela came running out of the coffee house at full speed and dove into Jacobi wrapping her arms around his body. They each grimaced in pain from this embrace, but they also didn't care about the aching discomfort their bodies were in. They each needed this moment.

"I knew you weren't dead. I just knew it. Thank god you found me," Angela said, holding Jacobi as tight as she could.

"I couldn't die on you. Not when we're having so much fun today."

"Yeah, there's that. But also, Vanessa is still waiting to be paid for my cappuccinos."

And she was. Standing there by the register looking at the 'domestically abused couple,' hugging one another.

"What do you think happened to them?" The mullet barista asked the other barista at the register.

Vanessa continued to chew her gum and rolled her eyes. "I don't know Sebastian, maybe they get real freaky in the bedroom. Did you notice his tie matches her eyes? That's real cute. That's a couple in *real* love."

V. Confrontations

Back in the car, Jacobi handed Angela her cell phone, knowing how badly she wanted to speak to her parents to tell them she was safe. While on the phone, Angela didn't get into specifics to worry her anxious parents. She told them they should stay in a safe place for just a little bit more time, as Jacobi focused on driving.

The streetlights they were driving so swiftly past were beckoning the buzzing insects towards their welcoming orange glow. The night air calmed Jacobi's sense of being. For the first time all day, he felt he was in control of his own destiny and wasn't running away from someone. As of now, he was running towards someone; the same someone that had apparently given him up, also known as, Mr. Hornsby.

For a few blissful moments, Angela felt safer than she had all day. She was sitting next to the man who was protecting her, and she was speaking to her parents who were her ultimate calming presences. She felt as if the worst was over, and wherever they were headed now, couldn't be worse than the safe house.

"You are safe here." *Yeah, my ass.*

The look on Jacobi's face was a bit frightful from Angela's perspective. She knew it wasn't about her, but she didn't understand why he looked so intense at this moment.

"Everything all right?" she asked, reaching for his hand. Jacobi took her hand and squeezed it.

"Everything is fine." He responded, giving Angela a quick smile. She didn't know Jacobi long, but she knew him well enough to know that smile was bullshit.

"You don't look like everything is fine. What's going on?"

"I just, I need—I have to do something right now that I honestly don't want to do."

"What are you talking about? What do you have to do?" she asked. Angela was prying, but this wasn't the time to keep secrets from one another. She needed to know what the plan was.

"When I woke up on the ground outside the safe house, my first thought was of you. I was so scared they had gotten to you before you made it to the panic room. I had confidence you would figure it out and you did, but I was still a wreck."

"I'm safe. And that's mostly because of you. You don't have to worry about me now. We made it out of there—beat up and cut to hell, but we made it."

"But that's just it. We almost didn't make it. And we were in my agency's safe house. So that got me thinking, how did those assassins find us? There was no trail."

"They seem quite resourceful. Rocket launchers and driving bulldozers through houses. They seem quite capable of finding us, somehow."

"But that's twice now. I can understand finding your location at the hotel. As much as we hid your identity and made arrangements so you'd be protected, they must have someone on their crew to acquire that information—but the safe house location? That's just too improbable."

"So what are you saying?"

"I'm saying there were only a select few people who knew the safe house's location. And those people were myself, Mr. Hicks, and Mr. Hornsby—my boss."

"The 'Mr. Hornsby' of Hornsby's Coffee House?" Angela said, quite confused, but putting all the pieces together.

"Yes. So if I didn't give the assassins the location, and Mr. Hicks damn well couldn't have given them the location, then it only leaves one man."

"And so we are headed to meet your boss, I take it. This is the something you don't want to do, but feel you have to."

"I'm meeting him, you are staying away from him. If he compromised us, you aren't safe to be around him. But, I have to know for sure, otherwise we're in more trouble than I thought."

Of course, Angela tried to argue with Jacobi about staying in the car while he confronted his boss, but she didn't win that argument. The drive took them an hour or so, all the while they spoke about different subjects, mostly first date topics. There was never an awkward silence between the two, and even a couple of laughs along the way. But the closer Jacobi drove to Mr. Hornsby's house, the quieter he became.

By this point in the night, Duke had driven to Angela's boss' home as well. Rocky was sweating bullets in the backseat, shaking as the drugs were starting to wear off. As Duke pulled up to Dr. Rayne's home, he handed Rocky the bottle of pills for the pain he was experiencing.

"Take a few more, I need your assistance in this," Duke barked. He didn't have the patience needed for a gun shot sufferer. He only had one thing on his mind and that was successfully kidnapping Dr. Rayne. He was the crucial part of phase two of the plan. Since chasing after Dr. Haven and her bodyguard was such a miserable failure for his team, he needed Dr. Haven to surrender to him.

Rocky put the bottle to his mouth and ingested quite a few pills from it. Crushing them with his teeth and swallowing a heavy amount, it only took a few minutes for his aggressive nature to come to life. He was jerking around in the backseat like a crack addict. Duke had planned to help him out of the car, but Rocky wasn't having it. He wanted to scoot out on his own, since he wasn't feeling any pain at the moment.

Duke held Rocky's face in his hands and went over the plan with him again; since the first time round he was too out of it to comprehend it. The pupils in Rocky's eyes took up his whole eye and Duke was almost taken aback.

"Are you up for this? You're my right-hand man now, Rocky. I need you with me on this." Duke pleaded.

"I'm here with you, boss. I have this. Wait right here and I'll be back in no time."

With a jump in his step, Rocky went around to the back of Dr. Rayne's home. There was a single light on in his house, coming from his home office. Dr. Rayne was working on his computer, and Duke was watching him through the window. He was on the first floor of his home, sipping on some coffee and typing away.

Unbeknownst to him, Rocky had made it inside, and was tiptoeing into the office. Duke looked both ways, making sure they were still alone on this street. When he looked back through the office window, he saw Rocky smash a glass vase over Dr. Rayne's head. At once, Dr. Rayne hit the floor and Rocky dragged his unconscious body out of the room. Once outside, Duke helped Rocky tie up Dr. Rayne and lay him in the backseat.

"Good work, Rocky. Way to be a team player even when you aren't feeling one hundred percent."

"Piece of cake," Rocky said with a smug smile on his face. "Hey, do you have any more bottles of those pills?"

"I do. I also have great news for phase two. While you were taking care of business inside, I spoke with Bows and Worm. They found a picture of Dr. Haven's ex-lover, Jeremy something or other. They are en route to his home to kidnap him, and bring him to us. If she wasn't coming for this guy, she sure as hell will come for this Jeremy guy. We'll have this bitch right where we want her."

"What about Boulder? You didn't say anything about him," Rocky asked.

"I didn't? Oh, he's with them too. He can't wait to see you. He's excited you're doing better."

Duke was lying, of course. Bows had updated him on Boulder's condition. He was in terrible shape, being shot in the rib cage, and a sliced up eyeball. He lost a lot of blood and if it weren't for Bows and Worm to patch him up after the safe house brawl, he would have died. They were in some shady motel for the time being, letting Boulder rest before making their way to grab Jeremy. Duke recognized if he told Rocky any of this, it would sidetrack his mission because Rocky was quite unstable, especially when it came to Boulder, or Bows. So he lied to him, and now they were on their way to their new destination.

Outside Mr. Hornsby's beach house, Jacobi silently prepared himself for the confrontation. He would never have imagined his boss betraying him like this, but this was the only explanation he could think of. Angela was practicing with the gun Jacobi had given her just moments ago. He wanted to teach her how to use it, in case they were separated once again.

He told her it was probably too big for her hands, but it would do the job if necessary. He taught her how to load it, how to aim and how to take the safety off when she was ready to pull the trigger.

"I don't want to shoot anyone. I'm not a killer," she said.

"You won't have to, but I want you to know how, in case one of these maniacs finds you again. I don't want you to be a victim. You should know how to defend yourself if I'm not there."

"Why wouldn't you be there?" she said, putting the gun down on the dashboard.

"I will be, I'm just saying it's good for you to know how to use it," Jacobi inhaled a deep breath squeezing his eyes shut. "I have to go in there now. Please, just wait for me here and do not come out no matter what you hear. Promise me."

"No. What if I hear gunshots? I'm not going to just—"

"Angela, please! Promise me," Jacobi demanded.

"Fine. I promise. But, this is stupid."

Jacobi squeezed her hand, looking her square in her eyes. He wanted to kiss her lips so badly right now, but this wasn't the time. He didn't even know if there would be another time for that. There was a connection brewing between the two, but he didn't know what to make of it and now wasn't the time to figure it out. He had business to take care of and Mr. Hornsby was on his right mind now.

Jacobi walked out of the car and made his way up his boss's driveway. Angela kept fiddling around with the gun, not being completely honest about her dislike in handling this weapon. She found it to be a much-needed distraction right now and felt a bit empowered being a bit more knowledgeable about these things.

Startled at the loud ringtone of her phone, Angela put the gun back on the dashboard. She looked at the screen of her phone and answered it at once when she saw it was William's number calling.

"Oh Will, you have no idea what my day has been like today!" Angela said, expecting him to ask her a million questions. But all Angela heard was muffled sounds coming from the other end.

"Angela! Don't come for me! Stay away! I—"

WHACK!

There was a solid thud after she heard William's breathy pleading coming through the receiver's end.

"Will? Dr. Rayne? Are you there?" she asked frantically.

"Oh, he's here, my dear. But he's suddenly unable to speak with you. I'm sure he'd love to see you in person though. How about you bring that sweet ass over here and meet with us? After all, we all have so much to discuss." Rocky said, laughing softly after speaking.

"Who is this? Please don't hurt him. We'll meet you wherever you are, please…"

"Don't worry about who this is. And there is no 'we,' that's going to meet us. We only want to see your pretty face. You better ditch that big oaf who's with you. Although, I'm sure I'll see him soon enough to put a bullet through his head."

"Please, let Dr. Rayne go. He has nothing to do with this!"

"I promise he's in good hands until you get here. If you come alone and meet us at the location I send you, nothing will happen to him. You better get a move on soon, and I'll be in touch where to meet us, pretty lady. Dr. Rayne is counting on you…"

Rocky ended the phone call and Angela sat in the passenger seat shaking.

What do I do now? This can't be happening. But, William needs me.

Wiping the single tear that was starting to form in her right eye, Angela unbuckled her seat belt and slid over to the front seat of the car. With her back still aching from the knife wound she had to sew shut in the panic room, she grabbed the gun off the dashboard and placed it in the passenger seat. She didn't start the car; she just sat there pondering what she should do.

After Jacobi picked the lock to the front door and let himself in, he noticed none of the lights were on. The home was quite dark, except for the moonlight seeping into the glass house. It was a cloudy night, so the light kept coming in waves creating shadows all over the walls. There was a distant thumping noise, coming from the upstairs floor.

Jacobi had armed himself with a couple of guns from the safe house, before pushing Ace into the caved in floor. That's how he was able to spare a gun for Angela. He kept his gun out in front of him, holding it with his good arm. Mr. Hornsby wasn't a fighting man, so he didn't have to worry about a hand-to-hand fight with him, but he did know how to shoot a gun.

As Jacobi made his way to the bedroom, the thumping sound got louder. Slowly, he opened the bedroom door and peered inside. He didn't expect to see Mr. Hornsby in this condition. He stepped inside the room and put the gun to his side. The thumping sound was Mr. Hornsby's legs hitting the bedpost every time the ceiling fan would spin around. He had hung himself on the ceiling fan and was slowly spinning around in a circle.

Jacobi walked up closer to examine him and it looked as though he had been dead for a couple hours. There was a single note on the bed with his name written on it. Jacobi picked up the note and read:

Dear Jacobi,

As you probably guessed, I'm not the man you thought I was. I regrettably betrayed you, and Steven, and I'm disgusted with myself. The man I gave your whereabouts to won't be finished with his mission to kill Dr. Haven, or anyone else in his way, until it's done. I'm sorry for my weaknesses and I hope you have it in your heart to forgive me. I don't deserve it, but I hope one day you will see how trapped I was.

See you on the other side.

Jacobi folded the note and placed it in his pocket. He walked down the stairs in a state of shock. He couldn't believe what he had just seen with his own eyes. The man he had looked up to as his boss and friend for so many years had committed suicide and admitted his betrayal. There would be no confrontation with Mr. Hornsby tonight. Jacobi walked out the front door and shut it behind him, making sure to wipe off the fingerprints he could have left. He didn't want any trace of being at Mr. Hornsby's home.

He didn't know what he was going to tell Angela. But, he didn't have to worry about that at the moment, seeing as Angela was gone.

She had taken off to be the hero for her boss, leaving Jacobi stranded at his dead boss's home. Jacobi called Angela over and over again, hoping there was some explanation for her disappearance, but she didn't answer. She knew if she did, Jacobi would convince her to come back and she couldn't be persuaded, not when her boss's life depended on her. After the tenth time calling, she finally answered.

"I'm sorry, Jacobi, but I had to leave. My boss is in trouble and they told me to come alone. You have to let me do this."

"Angela, get back here right now. Don't be insane! They'll kill you! If they really do have your boss, let me help you save him."

"They want me to come alone, you can't be there, or he's dead. I have to try. I...I just want you to know...I—I don't want you to blame yourself if something happens to me."

"Don't do this, Angela. Please, we can find another way."

"I'll see you soon, Jacobi." Her voice was shaking and tears swelled up in her eyes.

CLICK.

"Angela? Angela, are you there?...Fuck!"

CHAPTER 10

ANIMAL CRACKERS

I. Caged

Through their earpiece communication devices, Rocky and Bows were exchanging the sappiest words chatting about how much they loved one another. It was nauseating to the rest of the team listening in, as they were all on the same frequency forced to eavesdrop. Duke was trying not to pay them any attention, driving the stolen car to the abandoned zoo. This was the place he had envisioned Dr. Haven surrendering herself to Rocky if she wanted to see her boss alive. Lying unconscious in the back of this stolen car, was Angela's boss, Dr. Rayne, drooling on his shoulder. His wrists were tied behind his back and there was a solid bump on the back of his head, due to a vase Rocky had smashed on his head earlier.

"Baby, I will never scare you like that again. You never have to worry about your Rocky-bear."

"Would you two shut up, already? We're almost there and we need to be prepared for her arrival." Duke wasn't in the mood to hear the couple conversing about their relationship over the communication devices.

"Sorry, sir. It's all business from here on out. Hear that, baby? We're almost at the Old Zoo. Good luck with your operation, even though we won't need this Jeremy fella. I'm confident Dr. Haven will show up to save her boss man. And when she does, we'll kill this broad, once and for all. Over and out."

Duke grimaced in Rocky's direction, saying, "What'd I tell you about saying that shit? You sound like a goddamn fool."

"My bad, boss."

Duke was clearly stressed out about phase two of his plan. There wasn't supposed to be a phase two, but the first go around was quite a blunder of epic proportions. So, here he was, driving Rocky and the man he just kidnapped to an abandoned zoo in Griffith Park, Los Angeles. It was known as, the Old Zoo, and it was completely abandoned, except for the hikers and random visitors that frequented the grounds during the day.

The empty animal cages lined the park pathways, and during the daytime, children enjoyed pretending they were lions, or elephants, walking around on all fours, entertaining their parents. The walls inside the vacant cages were spray painted with artistic graffiti from all the years of teenaged-hoodlums coming by to cause a bit of mischief. Some of the graffiti was inappropriate, but most of it was creative and inspiring from artists with authentic talent.

At this hour of the evening, the Old Zoo was unoccupied and Duke knew this would be the perfect destination to trap Dr. Haven. She and her bodyguard had made a fool out of Duke's team of assassins and he wasn't going to let it go on any further. The Mayor of Chicago had paid Duke good money to get this operation done in a timely fashion. If Dr. Haven was not eliminated by dawn, it'd be considered a failure in his book.

Pulling into the parking lot, Duke took out a cigar and clipped the end of it. Once lit, he puffed on it until it had the perfect burn. This made Rocky think about smoking pot, so he checked his pockets for any left over joints he might've had, but found nothing.

Duke must've found and tossed my stash when I was being patched up. Damn it!

"You ready, kid?" Duke asked, still puffing on his cigar. The car was filled with ashen smoke and Rocky began to choke on it. Duke was the first to open his car door, slowly making his way over to the passenger side to help Rocky get out of his seat, but Rocky swatted Duke's arm away.

"I can do it myself!" Rocky bellowed, holding onto the wrap that covered his chest wound.

There was a dab of blood soaking through the bandages, but Rocky paid no mind to this. He recognized he was in need of more drugs if he was going to get through the rest of this night. At this point, the pain was too unbearable.

Duke could see the distress in Rocky's eyes, but he was proud of his determination to get out of the car on his own, even if he was in excruciating pain. He was proud of the discipline and willingness his team of assassins had for always ascertaining they were warriors ready for battle. They were never a disappointment to him, even when they were in terrible predicaments. Except for Ace, who was Duke's biggest disappointment, as of today.

When thinking over all the years Ace had been his right hand man, leading the team to victorious results in all the various missions, Duke felt a sense of frustration.

Where did I go wrong with him? How could he turn his back on me? I'll show him what happens to a man who crosses Duke Harrington...

Once Rocky managed to get his aching body out of the car, he followed Duke to the trunk.

"How the hell does this thing work? Open up, you piece of shit."

Duke was talking to the keychain contraption on the set of keys he was holding. Since he had stolen this vehicle, he wasn't familiar with the gadget that unlocked the trunk. With enough force of his thumb on the button, the trunk popped open and Duke showed Rocky what he had brought along with him.

Rocky looked inside the trunk and saw a wide assortment of weapons to choose from. Duke was never much of a weapons man, as he mostly handled the planning of the missions and the finances to cover the missions. Plus, he had a club to run, even if it was a front for his hidden headquarters. But even if he wasn't on the frontlines of these missions, he knew what his team appreciated—and that was, clearly, a good weapon to choose from when handling business.

Rocky's face lit up as he saw the Sais. He had always been drawn to them, even as a child. He mastered the weapon taking Jujitsu classes with his brother. Their hand-to-hand combat skills were fanciful and intimidating, but watching Rocky spin and twist the Sais around his fingers was an uncanny sight. He was a natural spinning them around, even as his chest felt like it was on fire.

"These will definitely do."

Duke closed the trunk, after grabbing a revolver for himself. Phase two didn't involve him being close by, but he thought it would be a good idea to arm himself, just in case things drifted off course again.

"This is it for the pills, until we get back to *Sway*. Be mindful of taking them. We don't want you falling apart out here in case things get serious." He said to Rocky, handing him the last bottle of pain pills.

Rocky opened the bottle and put three pills in his mouth. Duke turned away from Rocky to load the revolver and Rocky snuck a few more pills from the bottle swallowing eight pills in total. It would only be a matter of minutes before they started to kick in and that warm fuzzy feeling would return to his neck and face.

"Let's get into our positions. Call her again and get her ETA," Duke ordered.

He walked in the opposite direction of Rocky, with his revolver in one hand and binoculars in the other. Even though he wouldn't be standing with them openly, he would see and hear everything that happened when Dr. Haven surrendered herself.

And she was just minutes out at this point in time.

What the hell am I doing? I should turn back now and pick up Jacobi. But then they will kill William. I can't just leave him to die. I'm not a coward. They'll make a trade. My life for his—or, they'll shoot us both and we'll be dead. Shit. What do I do?

Angela was speedily driving down the back roads towards the Old Zoo. Rocky had given her directions and made her prove she was alone in the car using her camera. She gave him the finger and hung up on him after he gave her the last bit of directions.

The night sky was dark, except for a few airplane lights in the dense atmosphere. The pollution in the sky created a haze over the city's lit up stratosphere. Angela had the windows rolled down and the music cranked loudly. If she was going out tonight, she wanted to feel alive, at least for the remainder of the time she had left.

She looked at the many missed calls from Jacobi on her phone and felt a sense of sadness. She didn't know this man well, but she cared for him and felt horrible about stranding him at his dead boss' home. The text messages from Jacobi were pleading arguments on why this was such a bad idea. But Angela felt as if she had no choice in the matter. These psycho assassins had her friend, and she wasn't going to be the reason he was murdered. She couldn't live with herself if she didn't try to save his life.

But Angela didn't feel heroic. She felt scared, as anyone would while walking into a trap. Knowing she might not make it out of this abandoned zoo alive, she began to think about her life and how fulfilled she felt it had been. The tears in her eyes welled up, thinking about her accomplishments and the love she had experienced, but they didn't fall down her cheeks. She had been crying for several portions of this day and she was spent.

No more crying, Angela. Get yourself together. You're almost there. Be strong.

The zoo gates looked quite eerie from afar, and this propelled Angela to go with her gut and park further away than she intended. Walking down a white rocky path, she noticed part of the Old Zoo was lit up in the distance.

That's where they are. Deep breaths, you can do this.

The handgun that Jacobi gave her in the car was halfway tucked into her pants behind her back. It was loaded and Angela felt pretty confident about using it if the situation called for it. She didn't want to shoot anyone, but if it was William's life at stake, she hoped she would have the courage to pull the trigger first.

The ground underneath her flats crunched with each step, until the rocky road became a paved path. She passed numerous vacant cages and timeworn animals signs with graffiti spray-painted all over them. With each step, Angela made her way closer to the lit up area of the Old Zoo. She could hear faint music coming from there and it sounded like an ice cream truck's song. Angela made her way closer and figured she was headed to the merry-go-round, and once she saw it lit up and spinning in slow circles, her heart sank. She saw William tied to one of the posts attached to a wooden horse on the merry-go-round.

His black messy hair was matted down on the side of his head from a portion of dried blood. He was awake, but there was duct tape over his mouth, so he couldn't call out to Angela. The music was light and child like, but it sounded creepy to her in this particular situation. The lights from the ride created shadows over her face and around the zoo cages. The bars from the cages cast their shadows on Angela's face and she suddenly felt trapped; ironically, like a caged animal.

Angela felt as if she were walking in a dream. None of this seemed like it was actually happening, but when she saw William tied to the ride, she took a deep breath and ran over to him. Hopping on the moving merry-go-round,

Angela made her way to William and ripped off the piece of tape from his mouth.

"Are you okay?" Angela asked, putting her arms around her friend and colleague

"I'm fine, but you shouldn't have come for me. These men are going to kill you, Angela. Run! Just get out of here!" William shouted. But it was too late.

"You can't leave now," Rocky said, popping out from the other side of the merry-go-round. "Not when we're about to have so much fun!"

II. Lion's Den

Rocky had a big smile on his face, standing just a few yards from Angela and her boss. The blood spot on his bandage was growing slightly by the minute, soaking through the wrap around his chest. The more pills Rocky ingested, the better he felt and right now, he felt like an untouchable god. Some of the stitches had ripped and this was causing the blood to soak through.

Spinning the Sais in his hands swiftly and with ease, Rocky felt quite confident having these two at his mercy.

"I'm here. You can do what you want with me, but let him go." Angela pleaded in a stern tone.

Watching Rocky spin his Sais, she knew she should be intimidated, but all she felt was her rage for this man. Angela had enough of these unjustly attacks on her life today. She was done being these assassin's target for reasons unknown to her and if these were the last minutes of her life, she wasn't going to take any shit from this guy.

"What's the hurry? Dr. Rayne came all this way to see you and you already want him to leave? That's not very nice of you, Dr. Haven."

Rocky was playing with his food right now. He wanted to drag this moment out and make Dr. Haven recognize she had no power in this situation. Angela was barely paying attention to Rocky at this point, as she was tugging on the ropes that tied William's wrists to the post. Of course, Rocky didn't let her get too far in this act of desperation, running over to her and shoving Angela off the merry-go-round.

Landing on her hands and knees, Angela scrapped her palms on the pavement and fell over to her side. Rocky began to laugh and jumped off the merry-go-round before it turned away from Angela. His laughing enraged Angela even more and she knew she had this awful man right where she wanted him. She reached behind her back pulling the handgun out from the back of her pants, and pointed the barrel straight at Rocky's head.

"That hurt, motherfucker…" Angela said, glaring in Rocky's general direction.

Rocky panicked for a slight second, hoping Dr. Haven wouldn't have the guts to pull the trigger. He held his Sais above his head and backed up a few steps.

"I wouldn't do that if I were you, Dr. Haven."

"Why shouldn't I kill you? You and your cohorts have really pissed me off today."

"If you shoot me, you'll get a bullet in your head from one of my… what'd you call him? A cohort?" Rocky asked. "You didn't think I came here alone, did you?"

"I still ask you, why shouldn't I pull the damn trigger? You're planning on killing me regardless, right? Why shouldn't I take you out with me?"

"If you behave yourself and surrender to us, we'll let Dr. Rayne go. If you shoot me, you die and so does he." Rocky said this, hoping Duke would come out guns a-blazing, but he was silent on his side of the earpiece.

Angela's forehead was dripping beads of sweat down her temples and her palms were drenched; she didn't know what to do, or what to believe.

She figured this man was speaking the truth about not being alone, but she didn't believe they would let William go if she surrendered herself. Rocky was inching his way closer to Angela step by step, as the merry-go-round kept spinning beside them. William was trying his best to escape the ropes he was tied to the post with, but he wasn't getting really far.

"Don't come any closer, or I'll shoot you!" Angela screamed. They were just a few paces away from one another. Angela's hands were slightly quivering holding onto the gun. She had never shot a gun before, let anyone a person.

"I tell you what, how about we put our weapons down at the same time, and have ourselves a chat. Maybe we can work something out, together? What do you say?" Rocky asked, knowing all too well he had no intention of putting his weapons down.

His only goal was to get the gun out of Angela's hands, but she didn't fall for his false words. She kept her arms outward and continued to hold the gun arms length away from her, pointed right at Rocky's chest.

"Leave now, and don't come for us again. That's the only option on the table for you. Do not test me. I'm at my wits end with you people." Angela pleaded once more, hoping this man would come to his senses.

"Okay, I'll leave. But, you should know one thing first. I couldn't possibly leave without seeing the look on your face when I tell you," Rocky paused and leaned in closer to whisper. "We also have Jeremy, your ex-fiancé."

"What? No. You're lying." Angela shook her head furiously.

She would not give in to these lies.

But how does he know about Jeremy? What if they do—?

She didn't have the time to aim accordingly when Rocky came at her with a leaping sidekick. Rocky's foot hit the gun right as Angela pulled the trigger, firing off a shot that went flying right by Rocky's earlobe, missing him entirely. The force behind his sidekick knocked the gun right out of her hands and onto the pavement too far out of reach.

Rocky's next maneuver was falling to his knees and striking down upon Angela's foot with one of the Sais in his right hand, stabbing her in the middle of her left foot. The pain was intolerable and Angela's scream echoed throughout the empty zoo. Rocky stood straight up and held Angela up by the throat. The Sai was still stuck in her foot and she wanted nothing more than to remove it, but she was being choked by Rocky and couldn't breathe.

This is it.

There were no images or flashes of her life flying by her eyes as Rocky was squeezing the life out of her airway. There was only a sudden sense of panic and helplessness that Angela had never experienced before. She didn't want to die, but here she was with a Sai stabbed into her foot and her throat being strangled by this killer. She reached for his face trying to scratch him with all the energy she had, but she was drained and the merry-go-round music started to slow down and become distorted. The lights began to dim slowly and Angela thought this was the end.

She looked into Rocky's manic eyes and saw his grin get wider. He let go of her throat, and threw her on the ground again. Angela hit the ground hard, struggling to catch her breath. There was a red imprint of Rocky's hand around her throat from squeezing it so hard.

"You brought a gun to a knife fight, and you still lost," Rocky laughed hysterically. "Well, technically, it's a Sais fight, but that's still funny as hell."

Angela tried to regain her composure lying on the ground, but she was still coughing and gasping for breath. She managed to get on her hand and knees, thinking maybe she could crawl to the gun that was just a few yards away. She didn't have a chance to move even an inch before Rocky was right beside her. He grabbed her by the hair and pulled her head up. Reaching down, he grabbed the Sai and pulled it out of Angela's foot, resulting in another loud scream from Angela.

Putting the pointed edge of the bloodstained Sai next to her jugular, Rocky said, "Listen, I know that's painful. I don't blame you for screaming, but you really need to pay attention to what happens next."

Still holding her up by her hair, Rocky leaned down to her ear and whispered, "I know you weren't the asshole who shot me, but you are still the cause of all of this. So you get to watch your friend die."

Angela could feel a light breeze blow past her face as she heard Rocky grunt above her. She had her eyes closed, but she opened them when she felt Rocky's stance change above her. She never saw the Sai flinging through the air, but she saw where it ended up: directly into William's back. It was a direct hit, causing William to slide down the post and wince, muttering inaudible words. Angela cried out, but the damage had been done and when the merry-go-round came back around, William's body was lying against the wooden horse. He was dead.

"You animal…how could you?" Angela asked, sobbing into her hands.

Rocky let go of her hair and circled around her holding the Sai up to her head. He watched the blood begin to drip out of Angela's shoe with a sharp sense of smugness. He knew nothing was going to get in the way of his kill. After all, he was an 'Inevitable.' He was apart of the team that always accomplished their mission, not matter the cost. There was no one who could stop him now.

"If you're going to do it, just get it over with already!" Angela yelled, staring at Rocky.

If this was it, then she wanted him to look her in the eye as he killed her. She was sick of his tormenting games. She watched the merry-go-round turn, trying to focus on the music, feeling that familiar feeling of tears streaming down her face. She thought about Jacobi.

*I wish you were with me right now. I just want to look into
your eyes once more.*

BANG!

Angela felt a mist of water splatter on her face. She slowly reached up
and touched her cheek and looked at her fingers, which were now covered in
blood, not water. For a split second, she thought Rocky had stabbed her with
his Sais and she was couldn't feel the wound because she was in shock. But
then she realized it wasn't her blood that sprayed her face; it was Rocky's.

He had been shot in the pelvis. As a scientist with a medical background,
Angela knew some fun facts about the body. For instance, she knew there
was a cluster of nerves in the pelvis that made this area of the body one of
the most painful places to be shot. Rocky hit the ground hard, screaming
out in pain. The blood was leaking out of his pelvic region at a steady rate.
Wiping the remaining blood splatter off her face with the sleeves of her
blouse, Angela backed away from Rocky as he dropped the Sais to the
ground. She could see in his face how much pain he was in, and she felt
no sense of sorrow. In fact, she was glad he got what was coming to him.

Having no idea who shot him, Angela was scared the shooter had missed
her by accident and shot Rocky instead. She didn't want to stick around to
find out who had inadvertently saved her life, so she managed to get on her
feet and limp to the merry-go-round. Her left foot was throbbing and her
shoe was filled with blood, but she pushed herself to the edge of the ride,
and hopped on. The merry-go-round spun around halfway before Angela
hopped off landing on her good foot. If the shooter missed her and hit Rocky
instead, she would now be shielded from another shot. She hid there for a
moment, as she heard Rocky yell out for her.

This was her chance to get away. Without taking a look back behind
her, she hobbled to the walkway directly in front of her that led to another
path through the trees. This was the area hikers came to in the Old Zoo
for a nice nature hike—a path that wasn't suited for someone that was just

stabbed in the foot. But Angela continued on, knowing her life was on the line in this abandoned zoo. She grabbed her phone out of her pocket and dialed Jacobi immediately. He picked up at the first ring, letting Angela have it for deserting him.

"Can we discuss this when I'm not fighting for my life, please?" she asked, quickly telling him where she was.

He told her if she was in a condition to drive, to meet him back at Mr. Hornsby's home. He'd be there waiting for her. It took her quite a bit of time to get back to her car, since she was limping because of her foot, and also quite paranoid about being shot by an unknown shooter. She made it back, and quickly pulled away from the Old Zoo, never once looking back in the rearview mirror.

While Angela was staggering back to her car, Rocky was using his arm strength to pull himself to the nearest cage. He needed to sit himself up and try to stop the bleeding from the gunshot. The chest wound had split open again, so he was bleeding from both places. From a distance, he could hear someone's footsteps approaching. His head was turned away from this person, and he was in too much pain to turn his body to see who it was. He was just a few feet away from an old lion's cage when he saw the shadow of the person that must've shot him.

Rocky grabbed the bars to the cage and lifted his body up in a sitting position so he was now leaning against cage. He lifted his head up and saw his shooter. Standing with a sniper rifle over his right shoulder, was the man he hadn't seen since earlier in the day. The man that caused this disastrous day to occur: none other than, Ace.

"I'm not sorry for shooting you, Rocky. You killed Dr. Haven's boss. Not that I care about taking an innocent life, as I've been guilty of it as well. But, then you were going to kill her. And I couldn't have that. I'm also not sorry because, well, you're a dick."

"Takes one to know one…" Rocky said, trying to stop the bleeding by putting pressure on his pelvic wound.

"I guess it does."

"Are you just going to let me bleed out?" Rocky asked, hoping Duke would answer him on the earpiece.

But he didn't say a word. And Ace thought Rocky was directing this question to him.

"No, even though you're a rat bastard, you shouldn't have to suffer anymore."

"Help me, do something!" Rocky begged.

All he wanted was Duke to step up and call an ambulance or even shoot Ace in the head with his revolver. But Duke was hidden in the shadows, listening from afar, while watching the whole scenario go down through his binoculars. He knew Rocky was of no use to him at this point, and wanted to see what Ace's next move would be.

"I can only do one thing for you, man." Ace said, pointing the rifle down aiming it at Rocky's forehead.

Assassins have a code they live by. One of the codes is take a fellow assassin out if they're suffering a terrible death. Ace could've let Rocky bleed out, but he was considerate enough to shoot him in the head and end his suffering. Ace walked away from Rocky's dead body and off into the night.

When Jacobi had pushed Ace into the caved in floor, he was hurt and hit his head on the basement floor, knocking him out temporarily. He woke to a buzzing in his ear, and realized the communication device in his ear had switched back on. The fall caused the hardware to switch back to the frequency the rest of the team was on, so Ace heard the plan from Duke and Rocky. That's how he knew to come to the Old Zoo and take him out. Ace had a feeling Duke was around, but he knew he'd be too much of a coward to show his face and fight him. So he began to walk back to the motorcycle he stole (from the same neighbor's house that Jacobi had stolen a car from), and drove away from the Old Zoo.

Duke watched Ace walk away into the darkness and didn't hesitate pulling his phone out. He dialed Bows, since Boulder was most likely still resting from his injuries. A glimmer of the future popped into Duke's mind and he saw the light at the end of the tunnel. Phase two was just a means to an end to get to the grand finale.

"Bows, I have some bad news to report. I think you should sit down for this…"

III. Bite the Head Off

Jeremy's home was quite a mess. It wasn't because he was a slob; he was just a busy man, working as a pilot and having a family of his own. His wife, Jessica, was eight months pregnant, so she wasn't doing much cleaning these days either. They had just been thrown a surprise baby shower by Jessica's sister, which also contributed to their cluttered home.

Jessica's sister, Carly, was still around the house, helping the happy couple clean up after the guests had all left. The party had gone on a bit late, and Jessica was yawning. She wasn't used to being up past 11 p.m. these days. But she was a trooper, and appreciated the party. Jeremy was already putting together the crib because he was in such a good productive mood. This shower gave him all the fuzzy happy feelings and he couldn't wait to be a father.

The doorbell rang, and Jessica asked Carly to see who it was, thinking it was one of the guests that must have forgotten their purse, or something. While washing the remaining dishes in the sink, Jessica spotted a chocolate cupcake one of her friends had made for the party. There were animal crackers on each one, as her friend knew the jungle theme of her unborn baby's room. Jessica grabbed an animal cracker off the cupcake and bit the head off (as she always did as a kid) and chuckled to herself. That's when she heard her sister scream by the front door.

Running as fast as her swollen feet could manage, Jessica left the kitchen and rushed to the front door, seeing three individuals dressed all in black. The woman, with bows in her black shiny hair, had a knife to her sister's throat. The larger man, with a white bandage taped over his right eye, had a gun pointed at Jeremy's head. Jessica dropped the animal cracker to the ground, speechless at this horrifying sight.

"What's going on? Who are you people?" she asked, frightened at the sight of these weapons.

"Honey, it's going to be all right. Go back to the kitchen," Jeremy said, calmly.

He was scared, as he had never had a gun pointed directly at his face before. He stood up from the floor and went around the halfway put together crib. Bows spoke in a serene voice, hoping she wouldn't need to cut the throat of the woman she had her hunter's knife against.

"Everything will be fine, girls. We just need Jeremy to come with us for a brief amount of time," she said, locking eyes on Jessica's upset face. "Go back into the kitchen, lady."

"You aren't taking my husband anywhere. Get out of our house, now!" Jessica yelled. But she didn't say another word, as Bows moved the knife ever so slightly against Carly's throat, causing a little drop of blood to drop down her neck.

"I won't say it again. Go back into the kitchen, and count to 30. When you get to 30, we will be gone and Jeremy will be with us. If you or this woman here call the police or do anything else foolish, we will kill him."

"No! Please…"

"Then do as we say, and everything will be peachy keen," Bows said.

Jessica knew she didn't have much of a choice, as she backed up and turned around walking back into the kitchen. The tears were flowing down her face and she slowly sat down at the kitchen table to begin counting out loud. She made it to ten, and Carly ran into the kitchen sobbing into her arms. They hugged one another and heard the screeching tires of a car squeal out of the driveway. Running to the front window, they only saw taillights rush past.

Bows and Boulder had completed their mission. They had Jeremy in their possession and informed him he was going to see an old friend in just a short while. Worm was driving the car and he made eye contact with Jeremy, right before Boulder hit him in the head and knocked him out cold. Worm was startled by this, but kept his eyes on the road.

He knew where they were going, but he was hesitant about getting there. This whole day was an emotional rollercoaster for him and he couldn't handle much more of it. He wanted out. After this mission was finished, he would tell Duke he was out for good.

IV. Pure Fabrication

Pacing back and forth on the beach, Jacobi waited for Angela to return behind Mr. Hornsby's beach house. He was so angry with her for leaving him and putting herself in such a hazardous situation. He had plenty of time to think of everything he was going to say to her when she came back, but when the car pulled up in the driveway, Jacobi came running to the front of the house and saw the damage done.

Angela's neck was plainly bruised by Rocky's hands and the look on her face was devastating. She had experienced something she had wished on no one. She witnessed a loved one being murdered right in front of her eyes. Angela wasn't crying anymore, she just looked emotionless. Clearly, she was traumatized from the events that had taken place and all Jacobi could do was hold her once again.

Holding one another in their arms, they stood in silence for a minute, listening to the ocean waves hit the shore. It was soothing being under the moonlight not having to speak or fight. They just got to be in the present and for this minute, they only needed one thing: each other. When the minute came to a close, Angela was the first to speak.

"I'm a fraud."

"What?"

"Everything that has happened to me is because of me. I created Pure and this stupid drug has finally caught up with me. The whole thing is a sham. And now, people that I love are being killed because of it."

"What are you talking about, Angela? What's a sham?"

"Pure! The love drug isn't *really* a love drug, at all. It's all just a glorified accident."

"I don't understand what you're saying. You've been through a lot and—"

"Stop! Just listen to me, please! Two years ago, I developed a serum that was supposed to be for gorillas being physically abused. It was meant to create a bond between their companions, so they wouldn't worry about being attacked when mating. Geneco let me have full reign over this serum and by accident, we discovered it was more than just a drug to treat abused gorillas. It also created a neurotransmitter attraction in human brains that released a high dosage of chemicals like oxytocin and vasopressin that are main components of what we understand 'love' to be."

"So, you're saying Pure doesn't do what it claims?" Jacobi asked, trying to understand what Angela was scientifically speaking about.

"When we think of love, it starts with testosterone and estrogen attraction which in turn involves adrenaline, dopamine and serotonin. Pure is like a chemical compound of all of these mixed in a perfect formula that causes our brains to seek out who we chemically match up with best. It's like someone who is an obsessive compulsive, but for finding their idealized match."

"So, you're saying it does do what it claims."

"In a matter of speaking, but it's not a love potion. There's no magical activation involved. This is why it destroys lives. It's not really love."

"Who's to say the chemicals we react to isn't love?" Jacobi asked sincerely, wanting to fully understand.

"That man in the picture I carried with me, he was my ex-fiancé, Jeremy. He was my everything. We were in love; or at least, I thought we were. He sat me down one day and told me he was an awful person. I couldn't imagine why he would say this, as I thought he was the best man in the world. I was working day and night, as Pure had just hit the shelves. We never saw one another and our relationship was suffering. I didn't want to see it and I fought with him when he told me we needed to work on it. I thought he was just being, Jeremy. Typical worrier. He told me he was an awful person because he said he fell for our mutual friend, Jessica. He didn't love me anymore."

"Sounds like a jackass," Jacobi said, taking a seat on the front porch steps of the beach house. Angela followed his lead and took a seat next to him.

"He wasn't. I mean, yes it hurt that he fell for someone else, especially being a friend of ours, but he simply fell out of love with me. It happens everyday. I freaked out on him. I threw things, big things, at his head. I was a wreck."

"Anyone would be."

"He had bags already packed for a week and I was too oblivious to even notice. I was a mad woman. I chased after him when he left our house. I had a syringe of Pure in my hand and I tackled him to the ground. He looked at me like he didn't recognize me. I was on top of him, in the grass, holding a syringe to his neck."

"Intense…"

"To say the least. I had every intention of injecting Jeremy. I needed to prove we were right for one another. But Jeremy knew what Pure really was. I told him the truth when it was first in development for human trails. He just looked me in the eyes, as I held the syringe to his neck, not saying a word. We both knew, even if we both injected Pure, and by some chance of fate our bodies and brains were chemically in sync, it wouldn't mean anything. We both understand it wouldn't mean it was true love. It was just a chemical reaction that was manufactured to be love."

"So you didn't do it?"

"No, I jumped off him and walked back inside. Geneco made him sign a bunch of NDA documents agreeing he wouldn't speak about Pure or our relationship to the media. And we've only spoken once, since that night. He ended up marrying our friend, Jessica, and they're having a baby. I ran into them a couple months ago at a restaurant. We were all civil and, of course, I congratulated them on the pregnancy. But, it was odd to see him again."

"Do you still feel the same way? Are you still in love with him?"

"It took a while for me to get over him, and I'll always care about him but I'm not in love with him anymore. Thinking back at the relationship I have good feelings about it, but we've both moved on. So, I don't believe I'm still in love with Jeremy. I just miss him from time to time. I think I miss being in love, most of all."

"There's nothing else like it," Jacobi said.

"So, do you get it now? This is why I call myself a fraud. People all around the world want me dead and for good reason. I'm sure the drug I created has messed up a lot of lives. Maybe, I do deserve to die."

"Don't say that. Don't ever say that. You are an intelligent, beautiful woman that developed a drug that gives people hope. Sure, it might have some downsides, but what great innovation doesn't have some kinks. Your drug has brought so much love into this world. Don't ever be sorry for that."

"My boss was murdered because of all of this. He didn't deserve to die. I'm the reason he's dead right now. And now, Jeremy's life could be in danger."

"What do you mean?"

"That murdering son of a bitch assassin told me the rest of his team had Jeremy. I thought he was bluffing, but I've been calling his phone and he isn't picking up. I think he might've been telling the truth, Jacobi."

Angela had made it through this whole explanation without breaking down, but this realization was just too much for her to take. She hugged Jacobi, grabbing onto his shoulders and weeping into his neck. She looked up at him, and into his eyes and without thinking it through, they both went in for a kiss.

It might've seemed like an inappropriate time to lock lips again, but people do crazy things when their emotions are as erratic as both of theirs were at this time. Angela pulled away first, brushing the hair out of her eyes.

"I'm sorry."

"Don't be. If Jeremy was taken, we will know soon. They will want you to come to him, just like your boss, right?"

"I guess so. But what do we do until they reach out to me?"

"We wait."

And so, they did just that. Angela placed her head on Jacobi's shoulder as they stared off into the black sky listening to the ocean's sweet tranquil sounds. They each felt a sense of solitude and isolation from the rest of the world, which was a much-needed sensation, waiting for her phone to ring.

CHAPTER 11

IN THE CROSSHAIRS

I. Grave Danger

Since there were only two shovels in the back room of *Sway*, Boulder and Worm were tasked with digging the grave for Rocky. Bows and Duke helped in their own way by wrapping Rocky's body in a body bag (funny enough there were plenty of these in the back storage room of *Sway*), and carving a stone for his headstone. They weren't zombies about these tasks; they all felt the loss of their fellow warrior, or brother or lover.

Worm didn't actually see Boulder crying, but he heard the sniffles coming from his nose. He didn't dare ask if he was okay to keep shoveling, for he knew this was a necessary step for Boulder to have some closure about his brother's death. Boulder didn't say a word the entire time he was digging. Shovels full of dirt kept piling up beside the hole they were digging and with each shovel, Boulder's pain grew.

Duke's car headlights were the source of light in the black night for Worm and Boulder. Inside the backseat of the car, Bows kissed the cold lips of Rocky one last time. After zipping up the body bag, she crawled out of the back seat and walked over to spot under the tree where Duke was carving a watermelon-sized stone. Duke had no artistic stenciling ability whatsoever, so Rocky's name was written in shaky carved lines made by a hammer and a screwdriver.

Bows wasn't impressed. "That looks like shit."

"I get that you're upset, but I'm doing my best. It's harder than it looks." Duke said trying to defend his work.

"Give me the damn hammer. I'll do it myself."

Duke wasn't going to have a fight about this with Bows because he knew she was obviously quite upset about losing her boyfriend. He handed the tools over to her and traded spots with her. Most people would think it a bit odd Bows wasn't crying, but Duke knew better about these types of situations. He had lost quite a few people in his life and the way he handled it was different each time. Sometimes there were tears flowing immediately, other times he felt numb to any emotions for a long while until it became real, whereas other times he was enraged. This was how he perceived Bows to be feeling at the moment.

Angry and full of fury, Bows was silent in her task and began slamming the hammer into the screwdriver with concentrated precision. Boulder and Worm were about a quarter of the way digging Rocky's grave when Worm put his shovel on the grass and started walking to the back door of *Sway*.

In his deep tone of voice, Boulder asked, "Where are you going?"

"I need some water."

"Get back here. Pick that damn shovel up and start digging again."

Worm didn't want to make Boulder any more upset than he already was, but he was utterly parched from the strenuous task of digging. He wasn't the fittest man being behind a computer desk for majority of his days, so this was quite a feat for him, especially without water.

Duke stuck his neck out and said, "Let him go, Boulder. Bring back a few bottles of water for all of us, Worm."

"I can wait." Worm chimed in, hoping Boulder would appreciate his willingness to continue helping him.

Boulder held out his hand at Worm signaling him to stop in his tracks. "No—leave it. I'll finish this myself. I should be the one to do it anyway. He's my brother."

It would be pointless to argue with Boulder at this point, and they all knew this to be true. Bows took a second to stop banging the screwdriver into the stone and looked up at Boulder's face. They made eye contact for a brief few seconds, as if they were telepathically communicating with one another, and then continued to do their duties. Even though they technically didn't telepathically communicate, they both knew one another well enough to know what the other was thinking. They had made a silent vow to avenge Rocky—no matter what.

When Worm walked back with an armful of waters, he undoubtedly dropped all of them on his way back to the group. He tried handing a water bottle to Duke as he was smoking yet another cigar, but he acted like he didn't see this gesture and kept puffing away. Duke was standing close by the gravesite, which is where Worm put the water bottle beside his feet.

Worm dropped another bottle by the pile of dirt for Boulder, but he ignored the gesture as well. Lastly, Worm walked over to Bows and held a water bottle out in front of her face, but she didn't even look up at him. She just continued to fix the rough stenciling that Duke had butchered.

In between puffs of his cigar, Duke tried to get his team on the same page. "I don't want to rush this, but we do have to plan out the rest of this mission. It's essential that we get the job done, more than ever. For Rocky."

No one said a word. The team worked in silence for the remainder of the time spent constructing Rocky's gravesite. Bows did break the silence once, pleading with Boulder to change the bloody bandage over his eye, as well as the one on his rib cage from the shallow bullet wound. He hesitantly complied taking a short break from digging.

By this point, a few hours had passed and it was nearly three in the morning. The grave was dug out and Duke, Worm, Bows and Boulder all carried Rocky's body from the back of the car to the hole in the ground. Boulder climbed inside the hole he had spent hours digging and did majority of the lifting, placing his brother in his final resting place. He climbed back out and grabbed a handful of dirt from the giant pile and scattered it over the body bag.

Duke followed Boulder's actions next, and then, Worm. Bows was the last to grab a handful of dirt—something that was completely out of character for her—and scatter the dirt over her deceased lover. They all stood around Rocky's grave for a moment and said their goodbyes in silence. Bows grabbed Boulder's hand and they stood there together, even after Worm and Duke had walked away to give them some time.

Boulder wiped a single tear falling down from his left eye, letting go of Bows' hand. He picked up the shovel once more and began to cover his brother's body with the dirt from the hefty sized pile. Bows backed away and grabbed the stone she had been working on, and placed it at the head of the gravesite. Her emotions were bubbling at the service, but she had still not broken down. There was too much to get done in the coming hours for her to be destroyed by this. She needed her focus and the only emotion she would let herself feel was rage. And her rage was directed at one person: Ace.

He had been the one to murder Rocky – Duke had told her every detail about his final moments. She had helped Ace get away from Duke in the mausoleum, when she still had hope he could come back to the team and be one of them again. But now, she knew there was no chance for redemption on his part. The rest of the team knew this to be true as well. Ace was just as much of their enemy as Dr. Haven and her bodyguard were.

Once Boulder had finished placing the remaining dirt on the grave, he threw the shovel down and walked back inside *Sway*. Worm and Duke had already taken showers in the hidden headquarters locker-room to clean themselves of the sweat and dirt, and Bows was now doing the same. Boulder walked directly to the bar and poured himself a stiff drink. He sat there drinking, even as Duke warned him he would have to be sober in the coming hours as he was a crucial part of the final phase of the plan. Boulder didn't care what Duke was saying to him. He had just buried his only brother and needed a couple of drinks to ease the pain he was feeling. But like Bows, he had only one thing on his mind - terminating Ace.

He doesn't deserve to live. I'll make him suffer until I snap his neck.

Once Boulder had a chance to shower and change, the team sat together on the stage upstairs. Duke went over the plans he had in mind to take out Dr. Haven, as well as her bodyguard and Ace. His priority was Dr. Haven, but he knew Bows and Boulder were preoccupied with killing Ace just as much, so he included his demise in his plans. The first part of the plan was to get everyone to the final destination.

The first phone call would be to Dr. Haven; enlightening her his team did, in fact, have Jeremy in their possession, much like they had her boss. Duke discerned Dr. Haven would come running just like before, for she was a good person that couldn't allow another loved one to die because of her. He would tell her if she called the police, or brought anyone else into this, Jeremy would die. Of course, he expected her bodyguard to be close by and truthfully, wanted him to be there. After all, Boulder had unfinished business with this man.

The next strategic move was to get Ace to this party. By listening in to the last conversation Rocky had with Ace—before he shot him in the head—Duke had found out that Ace knew about their plan to meet at the Old Zoo from his communication device which was now working again. Therefore, Duke would just have to have a "conversation" with his team members about where this was all going to go down, and Ace would come, not knowing it was a trap.

When Duke's team was all changed, armed up and ready to go, he made the phone call to Angela. She needed proof Jeremy was still alive before she would agree to meet. Duke thought this was acceptable. He opened the cooler where the kegs and bottles of beer were kept in Sway, and there was Jeremy—still tied up, mouth taped shut and wiggling around trying to get free.

He made a face-to-face call to Angela, showing her Jeremy was alive. As relieved as Angela was, she hated to see Jeremy involved in this at all. He looked scared, as anyone would be.

"Where do you want me to go?" Angela asked.

Duke was pleased with himself he had predicted how willing Dr. Haven was to meet. His final phase of the plan was coming together.

"We want to show you the future of your love drug, my dear. Accordingly, we should meet at the place you created it. Meet at Geneco Inc. Jeremy will see you there in an hour, Dr. Haven. Don't be late."

When Angela heard this, she looked at Jacobi and knew something terrible was going to happen. She couldn't predict what, but she was afraid to meet at Geneco.

What did he mean by 'the future of your love drug?'

Jacobi heard the entire conversation and needed to arm up. He went through Mr. Hornsby's personal firearms collection and took what he needed. He also tried to gave Angela a small handgun to defend herself, if need be, but she refused.

Angela grabbed the gun out of Jacobi's hand and placed it back in the compartment. She went on to say, "If you aren't there to protect me, and it comes down to me having to shoot one of them, I'm a dead woman anyways. A gun won't help me, as I figured out at the Old Zoo. It's better if I don't have one, that way they can't use it against me if they knock it out of my hands, or something."

"At least arm yourself with a knife, then. We can strap it to your leg and they won't find it. You need some sort of protection. It could mean life or death."

Not needing any more convincing, Angela agreed to strap a knife to her calf, under her pant leg. But she also thought what was the point? The more she thought about it, she realized this could be her final hours on this planet. It all seemed to be too much for her, not that she'd let Jacobi know about her doubts.

She put on a brave face for him, but she couldn't help being real about what she was walking into. This assassin group outnumbered the two of them, and they had Jeremy as leverage. If it came down to saving Jeremy's life, or her own in this encounter, she would choose Jeremy.

Jacobi was now armed and ready. "You don't have to do this. I can go and save Jeremy's life. It's a risk, but I was hired to protect you."

"I'm pretty sure you aren't getting paid to protect me anymore, Jacobi."

"Doesn't matter. I won't let these monsters hurt you. There's got to be another way."

"This isn't about me anymore. It's about Jeremy's life and if I don't go, they'll kill him. You know it's true. I have to go. It's the only way he has a chance."

Angela was done with this conversation. She had made up her mind and sat down in the passenger seat of Mr. Hornsby's car. They decided not to take the stolen car anymore, just in case they were to be pulled over. Jacobi timidly sat down in the driver's seat and pulled out of the driveway, heading to Geneco Inc.

Ace was trying to find a lead on Dr. Haven's whereabouts, and was driving around the city streets on the motorcycle he had stolen. He really had no indication of where she could be, but he knew it was his destiny to find her again. He had saved her life at the Old Zoo from Rocky. Once he shot him in the head, he knew he'd be on the run the rest of his life. Duke and the rest of the team would never stop until he was as dead as Rocky.

This meant he would have to kill each of them first, so while he tried to track down Dr. Haven's whereabouts, he kept his communication device on the accurate frequency, waiting until there was any word from his former team. Ace heard Duke come onto the earpiece, right as he was about to give up driving around for the night.

The frequency was a bit fuzzy, since the communication devices weren't made for long range, but Ace could make it out. "Boulder, Bows...meet us at Geneco Inc. Dr. Haven has agreed to meet there so we can finally end this. We are meeting on the 21st floor, in the Cloning laboratory. Do you copy?"

"Yes, Boss." Boulder responded.

As did Bows, closely after. "I copy, sir."

Ace turned the bike around, and headed to the Geneco Inc. building, as it was a well-known place. He knew Duke would need Worm to shut down all the camera feeds and lock down the building making sure no one could get in or out. Ace was hoping he could sneak in stealthily, but he was more than an hour out of the way. It didn't matter how he got in, he was determined to find Dr. Haven and save her. He was also determined to take out every last member of his former team.

Duke and his team knew Ace was listening in and was stepping right into their trap. They had already been driving towards the Geneco building while they had this fake dialogue through the earpiece devices. Ace was correct in his prediction about what Duke would need Worm to undertake for the plan to succeed.

Duke pulled up to the Geneco building and didn't hesitate to shoot the guard at the gate. He didn't have time to create a backstory for getting into the building. A casual murder was much easier. The team helped Duke stuff the dead guard's body into the trunk of their car and they proceeded to park in the parking lot.

Bows and Boulder walked ahead of Duke and Worm as they all made their way to the side entrance of the building. Duke had the keys to these doors from pickpocketing Dr. Rayne, after Ace had left the Old Zoo. The keycard had worked and the doors unlocked, and now the team was inside.

Duke wanted to be inspirational to his team, and said, "You two know what to do. Let's bring this operation to a closure, once and for all. For Rocky."

Boulder and Bows nodded in agreement and went their separate ways from Duke and Worm. They both walked into the elevator and went up. Bows was holding an earpiece communication device in her hand, and because it had to be placed high above her reach, she handed it to Boulder. It was part of Duke's plan.

Worm had an uneasy feeling in his gut, and felt like he was going to vomit. His red mohawk matched the flushness in his skinny face. Duke was leading Worm to the center of the building on the ground floor. This is where they had the central codes for the building's security system and maintenance programs.

Walking at a brisk pace, Worm said, "Sir, before I get the codes to this building and shut down the elevators and so forth, I need to confess something to you. Not confess, per say, but...well it's just that...what I mean to say—"

"Spit it out, idiot. We're almost there."

"I need to resign. I can't be apart of the team anymore. Not with everything that has happened today. It's just time for me to call it quits. I am so grateful for everything you've done for me. I am. I just can't keep being this person. I'm not cut out for it. I don't think I ever was, to be honest."

Duke didn't say anything back to Worm right away; he just kept walking in a quietly. Worm was fidgeting with the countless gadgets he had brought along in his bag, waiting for any type of response from Duke.

And when they reached the central control room, Duke spoke up. "I'm sorry you feel that way, son. It's been an honor having you as a critical part of the team. It won't be the same without you."

Worm was relieved. He didn't know how Duke would take this sudden news, but he thought it wise to speak up now when Duke had so much on his plate. That way, he would be too distracted to try to convince Worm he was making a mistake. Worm was influential, to say the least; so he was pleased Duke didn't try to talk him out of it.

When they reached the central control room, they spotted the guard behind the desk. He wasn't watching the small televisions that showed the many camera feeds from the building. A book in one hand and a sandwich in the other distracted the guard from watching the screens. It didn't take any time for Duke to walk into the room, unnoticed, and shoot this man in the head. Worm was not usually in the field when these missions were taking place, so seeing so many innocent people killed directly in front of him was quite bothersome. He couldn't wait to be as far away from these people as possible once this mission was completed.

Duke dragged the guard's body into a small closet where the external hard drives were kept and Worm took over the controls. He used his laptop and plugged it into the system board to take over the building's controls. Duke ordered Worm to disable the elevators and lock all the exits in the entire building, except for the front entrance. He wanted to see his targets come into the building one by one. Once Worm had full control over the building to Duke's liking, he spun around in his chair and clarified everything was set.

With a smile on his face, Duke put his hand on Worm's shoulder and said, "Great work."

"Thanks, boss. I hope you don't have any ill feelings towards me about resigning."

"None at all," Duke said, squeezing Worm's shoulder. "On the contrary, I feel elated you felt comfortable to tell me how you felt. You should move on, Worm. Maybe, in your next life, you won't be such a sniveling, weak *worm* of a man."

Pointing his gun at Worm's forehead, Duke pulled the trigger and shot him twice in the head. Blood splashed the computer screens behind Worm's head and the televisions were covered in dripping blood.

Duke gazed into Worm's motionless eyes, and whispered in his ear. "No one quits my team."

He put his hand over Worm's eyelids and closed them. Just then, Duke's phone began to ring, startling him. He looked at the caller's number and it was none other than, Harold Richmond, the man who hired Duke and his team to kill Dr. Haven.

"Mr. Richmond, I told you not to call me unless it was imperative that you speak with me. Are you calling for an update?"

"No, I need you to cease this operation. I'll still pay you for your troubles, but I don't wish to proceed, any longer. My son, whom I was doing this for in the first place, is happy. I couldn't believe it, but he's actually back to his old self once again. He has taken this woman's love drug and miraculously found his true love. I couldn't possibly wish death on this woman now. Please, tell me it's not too late."

Duke was stunned to hear the words coming out of this man's mouth. Just days ago, this man was utterly angry at the world, and especially at Dr. Haven. He wanted her dead and paid a happy sum for the job to be finalized with haste. Duke was speechless and didn't have the words in his head to complete a sentence.

"Mr. Harrington? Are you there?" Harold asked.

"Uh, yes, yes I'm here. I'm just taken aback, sir," Duke could've told Harold the job hadn't been completed yet and this whole mission could've ended right then, but he was too far down the rabbit hole and had to see it through to the bitter end. "I'm sorry to say, the deed has already been done. Please wire the rest of my compensation by the end of the day. Good day to you, sir."

II. Ex Marks the Spot

The traffic was still flowing well at this time of the early morning, but as the minutes passed by and additional cars came onto the roads, Ace decided to drive through the back roads to get to the Geneco building. He spotted the towering building from miles out, as it was 30 stories tall. Being a participant of his former assassin team, Ace understood he would have to be clever about the way he entered the building. His fellow assassins would be on the look out and he couldn't have anyone detect him before he had a chance to save Dr. Haven—or take each of them out, one by one.

He parked the motorcycle on a side street and ran the rest of the way towards the building. Ace wanted to find a way to get inside that was plausible, but quick. It was still quite dark outside, but he did his best to take note of the building's entryways. He made note of a window-washer's platform on the side of the east exterior of the building, but it was hoisted to the highest floor. There was no way he could use the crane (holding the platform) to get into the building.

Every entrance of the building was locked and there was no way to climb into any of the windows. Ace didn't know if Dr. Haven was already inside, and realizing he couldn't waste any more time, he decided if he was doing this, he might as well be all in. There would be no stealthy maneuvering to break into this building; he was going through the front entrance without caring if his team knew he was here to play.

Ace sprinted back to his motorcycle and hopped on. He speedily drove it up to the front entrance and began to rev the engine. Little did Ace know, Duke was watching him from inside the control room.

Duke asked himself out loud, "What the hell is this moron doing?"

There was about 100 feet of pavement between the glass doors of the front entrance, and the front tire of the bike. He sped off like a demon from hell driving full speed straight towards the front entrance doors.

Duke continued to watch Ace jump off the motorcycle into a somersault landing, just in the knick of time before the bike crashed into the glass doors and collided into the front desk of the lobby. Before he was shot in the head, Worm had turned off all the alarms in the building, so there were no sounds but the breaking glass hitting the marble floor and the motorcycle coming to a screeching halt. Ace felt like an absolute badass walking through the open entryway, crunching the shattered glass under his boots.

Of course, Duke saw him as a complete buffoon. "The doors were unlocked, you horse's ass."

Walking towards the elevators, Ace could sense he was being watched. He didn't have his sniper rifle on him, but he was armed with a few pistols. He was ready for his team to pounce on him at the first opportunity they had, but he was also prepared to scuffle. He pressed the 'up' elevator button and waited for about 30 seconds until he realized the elevator was shut off.

Motherfucking fuck-face.

Ace walked over to the staircase door and shoved it open, hoping this staircase wouldn't be as hot as the church one was earlier in the steamy day. He had 21 stories to climb and wasn't happy about it.

He had climbed up eight stories by the time Angela and Jacobi arrived at the Geneco gate. The first discerning thing they noticed was the absence of a guard at the gate, so they drove on in with their eyes peeled. They parked in the first space, closest to the front entrance. The building reflected the shadowy early morning sky, as it was only about an hour before dawn.

The air felt sticky once again, and Angela briefly wished she were swimming in the ocean. But she came back to reality and understood this is where she had to be. Jacobi was a couple strides ahead of her, but they walked unruffled, towards the front entrance of the building.

As soon as Jacobi discovered the front doors were shattered and there was a motorcycle smashed into the front desk of the main lobby, he pulled out his gun, ready to face whomever had set this scenario up. Angela was close by his side, but he signaled for her to stay put, out of harm's way, as he examined this mess.

Everything was falling right into place according to Duke's plan. Ace was on his way to the 21st floor, and Dr. Haven was now inside the building. All Duke needed was her troublesome bodyguard out of the way. Right after he shot Worm, Duke proceeded to place a tape recorder in the elevator. Still in control of the building's elevators and programs, Duke opened the elevator door, surprising both Jacobi and Angela.

There were slight murmurs coming from the elevator and Angela asked, "What is that?"

"Stay put." Jacobi began to walk slowly into the elevator with his gun out. He wasn't going to take a chance being caught off guard by any of the assassins. Once inside the elevator he could hear the struggling noises coming from the above the elevator cover. He jumped up and pushed the emergency exit flap over, but he didn't see anyone above him. Angela was still in the middle of the lobby, waiting to see who was making these strange noises.

Jacobi and Angela made eye contact from across the room, feeling like something here wasn't right. Jacobi was about to step out of the elevator, but he heard the sounds again. This time the murmurs were much louder cries for help. He wasted no time in jumping up and grabbing onto the edges of the flap hatch, pulling himself up. He looked around above the elevator and only saw the cables that held the elevator. But then saw an electronic earpiece device that was the source of all the odd cries for help and murmurs.

The elevator doors shut without any warning and Angela ran towards the doors, but didn't make it in time. The doors had shut and the elevator was now on its way to the rooftop, with Jacobi stuck inside. Angela banged on the elevator buttons, but it didn't stop. She banged her hand against the closed doors, and watched the numbers escalate. There was no way of knowing which floor the elevator would stop at, so she couldn't go to the stairs until she found out.

But as she watched the elevator numbers click floor by floor, she heard a gun revolver cocking, and realized that she and Jacobi had walked right into the trap that had been laid for them.

With a commanding kick, Ace flung the 21st floor door wide open, gun out and ready to pull the trigger at any sign of one of his former associates. He held onto his cross with his other hand, praying for Dr. Haven to still be alive. Over the earpiece, he had heard this was the floor Duke had planned to meet Dr. Haven at, inside the Cloning Laboratory. So all he had to do was find this lab, and save the day. Seemed simple enough to Ace, especially knowing he had the element of surprise on his side.

Noticing the window at the end of the hallway was beginning to show signs of dawn's light, he walked that way first. He passed by a few rooms, but each room had the look of a boardroom, contrary to a laboratory. Ace made it to the end of the hallway, passing each separate room along the way and none of the rooms remotely resembled what he pictured a cloning laboratory would look like.

Ace took just a small moment for himself and looked out the giant glass window. Still holding onto the gun with his right hand, he felt the cold air-conditioned glass with his left palm and removed his hand from the glass. He stared at his palm print slowly fading into evaporated matter when he felt the stinging sensation of a large knife being plunged into his back.

Before he knew what had happened, Ace heard a familiar voice. "That's for Rocky."

Biding her time just right, Bows had hopped down from an air vent in the ceiling tiles to make her move. There would be no gun battle between the two ex-lovers, as Bows foresaw how that would've ended up for her. So she knew she only had one chance to attack Ace in a devious manner, and she took it. It wasn't honorable, and it was definitely against an assassin's code, but she stabbed him right in the back like the cold killer she was.

At first, Ace didn't realize how bad the stab wound actually was, until he turned around trying to reach for the knife, but couldn't grab it. It was just an inch to the right of his spine, and had barely punctured his right lung. Bows had the upper hand at this turnaround and grabbed his hands, holding the gun above their heads.

Ace used all the strength he had to try to hold onto the gun but his grip was slipping, due to the intense sweat coming from his palms. He knew if he didn't do something fast, Bows would get the best of him. Using his body weight, he backtracked into the wall behind him, and using his left foot against that wall, he propelled himself and Bows into the opposite wall. The gun slammed against the wall and fell out of his hand. Bows bent over to pick it up but Ace grabbed her by the neck and flung her between him and the window.

Time slowed down and Bows looked into his eyes. She knew she was cornered now, but Ace still had the knife in his back and if she could just grab it and twist it, she could regain control over this battle. But as time trickled back to orderly speed, Ace made a last ditch effort purely driven by his adrenaline and did a 180 degree-spinning kick landing his right foot into Bows' chest, knocking her into the window.

These windows were sturdy, but Ace's kick was too powerful and when Bows hit the glass, her body smashed into it and she screamed the entire 21 stories down to her death. Ace fell to his knees, trying to catch his breath, hyperventilating at this point. He crawled to the edge of the hallway and looked down at Bows' body, sprawled out on top of a pool of her own blood. The window had completely shattered, except for a few shards of glass that hung onto the edge of the building and attached to one of the shards was the bow she had in her hair. It blew away in the light breeze that Ace felt on his sweaty face. Collapsing on the floor, everything went black.

DING...

The elevator door opened to the rooftop, and as Jacobi walked out, he saw nothing but an empty rooftop. Standing on top of elevator hub, Boulder looked down on Jacobi as if he were a zebra in a lion's territory.

Just a moment ago, Boulder was standing at the edge of the roof, looking down onto the ground. He had, of course, heard the screams from Bows as she plummeted to her death. Looking down upon her dead body, Boulder comprehended this was the end; not necessarily for him, but concerning him and the bodyguard, one of them was not escaping this rooftop alive once he arrived.

And not ten seconds later, the whizzing of the elevator alarmed Boulder into getting in position above the elevator hub, ready to spring on his prey.

Boulder was a large man, and when his full body weight landed on Jacobi's back, his knees gave out and Boulder tackled him face first into the rooftop surface. This caused Jacobi's gun to pop off two shots, before he was flattened like a pancake. As Boulder was still on top of Jacobi, he tried to wrestle the gun out of his hand, but Jacobi refused to let go. He fired off another three shots into the air, managed to get his left arm free, it was still hurt from being dislocated, but it was strong enough to poke Boulder's other eye, temporarily blinding him.

Jacobi hit Boulder in the rib cage where he had shot him, and Boulder gasped in pain. He leaned over holding onto the bruised wound, and swung his arm around knocking his fist into Jacobi's jaw, upper cutting him. Jacobi went flying in the air, landing on his back. Jacobi was in critical pain, but he crawled to his gun, as Boulder ran to the opposite side of the rooftop.

Still dizzy from hitting his already swollen head into the rooftop surface, Jacobi fired off the rest of his clip trying to hit Boulder but he missed every single shot. At the very least, this gave Jacobi some time to recuperate while Boulder was at the far edge of the rooftop.

Boulder laughed a hearty chuckle. "Not a very good shot, are ya?"

"I recall already shooting you once today, you oversized jamoke!"

"We all get lucky, sometimes. Too bad, Jeremy won't be."

Jacobi took a second to gain his composure and try to stop the ringing in his head. He noticed Boulder was staring at something right off the rooftop. It was a window washing lift, and Jeremy was tied to it. His mouth was gagged and his wrists were handcuffed around the lift.

Jacobi couldn't see Jeremy from where he was at, but he knew from the boom mechanism, that Jeremy was on the lift. Boulder didn't waste a second as he started the electric saw and began to cut the wire cables holding the lift to the rooftop boom mechanism. Boulder was laughing uncontrollably, and Jacobi had one shot to save Jeremy's life.

Boulder was at a disadvantage because of his sliced eye, he wasn't aware of his surroundings as well as he usually would be. Jacobi was still on the rooftop surface, not able to move much due to his injuries, but still not completely immobile. He did play this up for Boulder, pretending he was close to passing out, when he slipped a small circular tube out of his jacket pocket. This was one of the weapons he had gathered from Mr. Hornsby's home.

It was a small-scale blow dart gun from Mr. Hornsby's personal collection. Jacobi had always admired it ever since he had brought it back from Peru, and wanted to give it a try. But Mr. Hornsby had always told him it was a gentleman's weapon of choice, and Jacobi was no gentleman. It was ironic thinking of it now that he knew Mr. Hornsby had been the one to betray him in a not so gentlemanly manner, but he didn't let that distract him at this time.

He would only have one shot at this, and he had to nail it. He had loaded the dart prior to taking it from his boss's home, but there was only one. If he messed this shot up, he would be out of options. With his dominant eye, Jacobi took aim wrapping his hands around the tube directly in front of his mouth. He filled his cheeks with enough air to propel the dart across the rooftop, and exhaled sharply.

Boulder had just cut the second wire cable of the lift, and Jeremy was sliding around, almost falling off the lift completely. By the time he looked back at Jacobi, the dart had flown at a top speed and made contact with Boulder's chest. He felt the small prick of the needle in his chest, stopped the electric saw to free both his hands and pulled the dart out, dropping it on the rooftop.

"Make that twice today," Jacobi shouted in Boulder's vicinity.

Boulder was standing on the rooftop edge while he was cutting the wire cables. This was clearly a bad place to be standing, when a dart so powerful it would knock an elephant out makes contact with the intended target resulting in the poisons to seep through the veins and cause an immediate cardiac arrest. Grabbing his chest due to the extreme pain he now felt, he lost his balance and fell backwards onto the lift.

Jacobi managed to get to his feet making his way over to the edge of the rooftop where the lift was now hanging by one solid wire cable and another that was frayed and about to snap. Boulder was shouting in pain, writhing around causing the cable wire to fray faster with all the weight now on the lift. It only took a few seconds for the third cable wire to fray completely and snap causing the lift to hang by a single wire.

Boulder fell to the opposite edge of the lift and held on with both hands. Jeremy was handcuffed to the opposite side of the lift, trying his best to slip his hands out of them. Jacobi knew it was just a matter of time before the last cable wire snapped and the lift fell to the ground, so he made the decision to climb down the wire cable and onto the lift to save Jeremy.

There was only one way he could manage this in time. He needed Boulder's help. Using the lift's walls, Jacobi slid down to the side of the lift that Boulder was hanging from. His face was flush and his pupils were dilated to the maximum.

Jacobi took a chance. "You're going to die. The poison in your veins is heading straight to your heart and it will happen no matter what you do. But you can die either as a hero, or a villain. Give me the key to his handcuffs."

Boulder had predicted one of them wouldn't be leaving that rooftop with their lives, he just didn't expect it to be him. He thought about his brother and Bows. This mission had killed them, and now he was to be next.

"Please. We don't have much time! I need the key!" Jacobi begged.

Boulder had a good grip with his right hand, so he let go of the metal bar he was holding onto with his left hand and reached in his pocket. He grabbed the key and placed it in Jacobi's hand.

Before letting go of the lift due to his heart bursting, Boulder's last words were, "If I had to go out, I'm glad it was by your hands. You're a worthy warrior."

Jacobi watched Boulder fall to his death. It happened in slow motion, but at the same time, quite suddenly. He didn't have to watch his body hit the ground, for he could hear the end result, even from way up on the rooftop. There wasn't time to process this because he had to quickly maneuver his way back to Jeremy.

The last remaining wire was bouncing back and forth and fraying due to the constant weight it had to hold up. Jacobi's hands were shaking as he looked down at the ground at the two dead assassins. If he dropped these keys, Jeremy would be the next dead body down there. And if he didn't manage to get off this lift when it fell, he'd be the fourth.

The handcuff key slid into the lock and Jacobi turned the key, unlocking the handcuffs. Jeremy removed his gag and held onto the lift for dear life.

"Follow me, Jeremy. We're going to be okay!"

"I can't do this! I can't climb that thing!" Jeremy said, panicking.

"You have to. You're going first." Jacobi grabbed Jeremy's arm and pulled him up from the lift and onto the cable wire. Jeremy succeeded in his climb, although he was climbing slowly. Jacobi followed him up close behind, but heard the wire snapping inside the cable.

There was a loud cracking noise and the lift snapped off from the wire cable, falling to the Earth just barely missing the bodies of the deceased assassins. Jeremy made his way to the rooftop ledge and climbed over. Jacobi quickly followed. They sat against the ledge catching their breath and looking up at the morning sky. During their time on the rooftop, the sun had peaked out above the horizon and lit up the clouds in the sky.

"You see that one, there? It looks like a monkey playing a flute." Jeremy said, pointing at a random cloud cluster. He started laughing to himself.

Jacobi didn't understand what he was saying and didn't really care. He knew he had to get back in the building and get to Angela. Her life was on the line.

I'm coming, Angela… wherever you are, just hold on…

III. What's in a Name?

"Little fact about me, I've always had a phobia of elevators. I get claustrophobic and I panic because I get all choked up and can't take a breath. You ever have that feeling? You know, like you're trapped and there's no way out. It's terrifying." Duke was speaking to Dr. Haven, holding his pistol against the back of her head.

They were waiting for the elevator to come back down to the lobby, so they could take it back up to the 21st floor. For the few minutes of interacting in the lobby before this point, they spoke very few words to one another—mostly because they heard the sound of Bows' body hitting the pavement. Duke told Angela to come with him outside the building to check out what had happened. Once he glanced at the body and discovered it was Bows lying dead on the ground, he knew part of his plan had failed. Bows was supposed to kill Ace, not the other way around.

While Duke paid his respects to Bows by closing her eyelids, Angela spotted a man hanging on the window-washer's lift attached to the rooftop. It was hanging by three cable wires at this point, and swaying back and forth. She could see another man standing on the rooftop ledge, but she couldn't make out who it was. The sun was beginning to peak just above the horizon so her vision was a bit limited, especially since she was looking at figures 30 stories above her.

But Angela had a terrible feeling the man hanging off the right side of the lift was Jeremy. Her gaze was broken when Duke grabbed her by the arm and pulled her in front of him.

Duke wasn't paying any attention to the rooftop. "And we're walking back inside. Step to it, Doc."

He was already thinking about Ace being loose in the building. He didn't want any surprises from him, so he would have to investigate what happened up at the 21st floor. He pressed his pistol's barrel into the back of Angela's head and walked her back inside over the broken glass doors and into the lobby.

That's when he gave her his passive aggressive elevator jargon. Angela couldn't concentrate on Duke's words. She was too worried about Jeremy and Jacobi. She knew Jacobi was on the rooftop because she was watching the elevator come back down from the top floor.

The elevator doors opened and Duke pressed the pistol against Angela's head pushing her inside. Once inside, Angela stood against the left side of the elevator wall and stared at Duke, who was nonchalantly standing against the opposite wall.

Angela wanted answers. "Why are you people doing this to me? Who hired you?"

"Oh, my dear, it's honestly not important at this point. People want you dead all over the world. Your precious love drug was the worst thing that's ever happened to this world. Giving people an unreliable hope to find their special someone? It's fantasy. There's no such thing as true love, and you know it."

"I know I care about that man up on the rooftop. And I know you have the power to help him. Jeremy doesn't need to die over this. You have me, you don't need him."

"He might survive, I don't care one way or another about his life. What I really care about is my team and now they're all dead except for one."

"That's not his fault, or mine for that matter. You all came after me, remember?"

"That pesky bodyguard of yours is really something. If I didn't have to kill him, I'd want him to join my squad. He's quite the talent."

The elevator doors opened at the 21st floor and there was a trail of blood on the floor from the elevator to the shattered window across the hallway. There was a light breeze coming from the open window, reaching the sweaty faces of Duke and Angela. He pushed her in front of him and made her lead the way down the hallway. Angela walked slowly, hoping to delay the inevitable.

"Ace…where are you, son?"

Duke was peering his head into every door of each room along the hallway. At first glance, Duke was certain Ace had escaped this floor, since there was a trail of blood leading to the elevator doors. Except, there wasn't a smidge of blood in the elevator. This was too suspicious for Duke to reasonably prove one way or another if Ace was still lingering around on this floor. Angela had reached the end of the hallway and was stepping into a small puddle of blood by the broken window.

The sun was further up above the horizon and lit up the building with a shining bright orange glow. Looking out the window, she knew what Duke wanted her to do.

"I believe my mission leader has a crush on you, Dr. Haven," Duke began to say, still pointing the gun at Angela. "I'm not sure if he's still with us or not, but I'm pretty sure he will show his self-righteous face to save your pitiable life. So, I want you to jump."

Angela had predicted correctly. This insane man wanted her to jump out of this window and fall to her death. She took a step forward and reached the ledge of the hallway. Turning around, she stared into the eyes of the man that wanted her to jump.

"I won't do it."

"Then I'll shoot you dead, right here; although, it would look better as a suicide. Imagine the headlines: The marvelous Dr. Haven's suicide. Loved and Lost. It will be spun as a romantic Romeo and Juliet story. The love of your life died at the hand of assassins who were after you, but being the cause of his death, you didn't want to live anymore! And so you jumped."

"No one will believe that. You're a deranged psychopath," Angela didn't hold back. She obviously wasn't going to talk this man out of his plan, so she said what was on her mind even if that meant being shot dead.

"So you're going to choose a bullet in the head? It's your call. I'm just saying, maybe you'd like to take the rest of your life into your own hands and do us all a favor."

Coming down from the same vent that Bows had, Ace lowered himself with both arms and landed softly on the ground. Angela tried her best not to look at this man floating down from the ceiling air vent, holding his finger up to his mouth as a signal to not say a word.

"Fine. I'll do it," Angela said, now using a few seconds time to stall. She didn't understand who this man was, but she had a feeling he was this Ace guy that Duke was looking for. She didn't know his story, but there was something about the way he looked at her—something in his eyes that was just so familiar. She turned her back to Duke and the other man, standing behind Duke, and stepped to the utmost edge of the hallway, looking down on the dead bodies below her.

"That's a good girl," Duke said with a smile.

And then Ace took a small step towards Duke, inching closer, but mistakenly stepped onto a piece of broken glass alarming him straight-away. Duke spun around and fired his gun directly into Ace's chest. Right as the gun went off, Ace lunged into him, slamming his trusty pocketknife into Duke's neck. Everything was happening in a split second. Duke hit the floor on his knees as his eyes flickered and the blood spurted from his carotid artery. He fell onto his back and died in a pool of his own blood.

Ace fell against the wall and slid down onto his side. Angela came rushing from the window's ledge over to the man that had just saved her life. She didn't think about her foot still being in excruciating pain, or the stab wound in her leg. None of her injuries were a nuisance as she ran to this man's aid.

She knelt to his side and held him up in her arms as best she could. Ace was still conscious, but he was fading fast. The stab wound in his back was already causing a massive amount of blood loss, but this gunshot wound was worse. He looked up at Angela's face, as she was silhouetted by the golden sunlight that was shining through the hallway.

Ace was the first to speak, gulping in little breaths of air and exhaling faintly.

"There you are…"

"Here I am…" Angela whispered in response.

"I've been…trying to look into your eyes…all day. They're so… beautiful."

Angela smiled warmly, staring back into this handsome man's brown eyes. She held his head in one hand and his upper body with her other. His eyes focused on hers, and Angela knew there wasn't much she could do to save his life. She put pressure on the gunshot wound, but she could feel blood seeping out of his body at a rapid rate.

"I need—to say…one thing, before I go to sleep…" Ace's eyes kept shutting, but as he spoke to Angela, he looked right in her eyes and said, "I love you."

Angela was taken aback. She didn't know this man, but she also couldn't let him die without saying what he so desperately wanted to hear from her lips. Right as she opened her mouth, she understood everything. This man was a part of the assassin crew. He took Pure. He was in love with her and saved her life because of it.

Angela didn't have time to process all of this. It was too much for her to take in, so she did the only thing she could do.

"I love you, too."

Ace smiled back at Angela, reaching for the hand that was holding up his head. Putting his head on her lap, Angela let Ace hold her hand.

"I just need to shut my eyes…for one second," Ace said, closing his eyes for the last time.

"Wait, what's your name?" Angela tried to wake Ace up, but he was unresponsive.

Coming down the staircase, Jacobi had checked every floor and finally reached the 21st floor. He peeked his head in, and witnessed Angela holding onto this man's body. The same man that he pushed into the caved in floor, after he had told his far-fetched story to Jacobi. Jacobi stood in the hallway, giving Angela some space. She was crying now and bellowing into the man's face.

"You can't go yet. I don't even know your name…I don't even know your name…"

Jacobi made his way over to Angela and put his hand on her shoulder. She looked up at him, and then back at Ace's face. She was sobbing now and wouldn't let go of Ace's body for a few moments.

When she was ready, she placed his head on the floor and walked with Jacobi to the stairwell doors. Jeremy was waiting in the stairwell, leaning against the wall. When he saw Angela come through the door, he immediately grabbed her and hugged her. She was still in shock from everything that had just happened to her, but she hugged him back.

Jeremy suggested taking the elevator back down, but Angela refused to walk back into the hallway to get into the elevator. They all agreed to walk down the 21 flights of stairs together.

They reached the lobby without saying a word. Jacobi and Angela—and even Jeremy—had all been through too much for a sensible person to handle in one day. They had survived, but just barely. As they walked out of the Geneco building, they heard the faint sounds of ambulances and police cars driving towards their vicinity. Jacobi mentioned he had called them once he and Jeremy made it off the rooftop.

They each stepped into the ambulances and were patched up by the paramedics on the way to the hospital. Jeremy's wife was waiting for him when they arrived and Angela waved hello to her. Jessica waved back, as Angela was taken to a hospital bed. The TV in the hospital was airing news on a deadly shootout at the Geneco Inc. building. Angela shut the TV off, not wanting to be in that moment any longer. She looked over at Jacobi in the next hospital bed and they both smiled at each another.

Before falling asleep, Angela thought about Ace. She had never taken Pure, but if she had, she would have felt the same loving feelings he had felt for her, even if she knew it was just a chemical reaction fooling her mind. She was already distraught about his death, but now she thought about how she wouldn't be alive if he hadn't taken Pure.

Would he have saved me, or been the one to kill me?

Going through all the scenarios in her head, she stayed awake a bit longer than Jacobi, who passed out quickly due to the calming drugs in his system. They both needed time to heal their bodies from the day's events and left together the next morning. Angela wasn't ready for the media frenzy waiting outside.

Thinking about how fresh this story was on the news, Angela knew she couldn't possibly go back to her home, at least not right away. So she told Jacobi she needed to be with her family for some time and she would see him soon. She took the next private flight to her parent's home on the east coast, leaving Jacobi to ponder what the future held.

IV. Full Deck

It had been two months since Ace died in Angela's arms and about a month since the truth came out about Pure. After everything that happened that day, Angela took a much-needed retreat to her parent's home and decided the world deserved to know the reality about her love drug. She did countless interviews and set the record straight. Everyone in the world had different opinions about Pure and about Angela now.

Some people respected the fact she was honest about what the drug truly was, whereas others felt deceived and questioned the love they had for their "true loves." In the interviews, Angela expressed she wasn't a magical witch that created a love potion. She explained it was a chemically-based formula that was triggered by sight. Pure was taken off the market and once again, people were left to fend for themselves in the hunt for love. As for Dr. Angela Haven, she was the happiest she had been in years. She was back in town and reunited with Jacobi.

Jacobi and Angela were sitting on the same boat dock where they were nearly blown up by a rocket launcher. The old man stayed away from them when they came in to rent a boat. He didn't want to get pushed into the water by one of their hoodlum friends again.

Playing a card game on the edge of the dock, Angela put down her last card. It was, of course, an ace. She won the game and celebrated her victory. Jacobi playfully wrestled with her and she landed on top of him pushing his arms onto the dock. They were laughing and smiling and having a fun time.

Angela stood up and stretched her body, enjoying the warm sunlight. She turned her head to look down at Jacobi who was gathering the cards for a rematch, when she decided to splash him with some water from her foot.

Jacobi was soaked. He warned her, "Do it again. See what happens…"

And she splashed him with her foot again. Jacobi jumped up to his feet from sitting on the dock and flirtatiously chased Angela off the dock's edge. She dove in the water headfirst and he followed her by doing a cannon ball into the ocean. He found her underwater and took her in his arms, kissing her. They didn't know what the future would bring. All they knew was that they felt something for one another and that they had gone through an extreme experience together.

Without Pure's influence on the love market, people chose to date one another once again. They chose to be with someone, even if their friends or their mother disapproved. People made mistakes again and fell in love with people they probably weren't meant for, but that was the whole point. That's what Pure took out of the equation—the unknowingness of it all. The most crucial and exciting part of anyone's love story.

Nothing was for certain, but people did find love on their own again, even without Pure's chemically induced help. As for Angela and Jacobi, they seemed to be on the road to happiness. They took their time falling in love, one day at a time. After all, love *at first sight* didn't exist. Right?